Van Scott Drenn

An ordinary guy and a political cartoonist gal.

George E. Boyer

Printed in the United States of America.

ISBN – Paperback: 9798860558403

Library of Congress: TXu 2-387-691

Book design by Anna Zubrytska

Cover design by John Ryan

Table of Contents

About The Book

A lonely Laurinburg police officer named Ian Scott Drenn meets a beautiful political cartoonist named Kaitlin Lawrence when she does a good deed for the day.

Kaitlin marries Sean Morris, a schoolteacher, only to have their worlds turned upside down. An astute Laurinburg lawyer solves this crisis, but Drenn breaks Kaitlin's ankle to win her heart.

This is a work of fiction.

Acknowledgments

This book is dedicated to Tina, Cindy, Thomas, Richard, Tabitha, Douglas, Paris, and Deidra for being who they are. And Kaitlin, wherever you are.

Lend me your ear, 'cause my time is near,
I do not fear.
For all is right; my love for you is bright,
I still see the light.
Lend me your ear, 'cause my time is near.

Chapter One

dward and Susan Drenn were extremely proud of their son, Ian. They had arrived at Richmond Technical College early on Friday afternoon to see Ian graduate with an associate degree in arts in Recreation and an associate degree in science in Law Enforcement.

Edward Drenn had graduated from the University of Indiana cum laude, and he played professional football for the Cleveland Browns for seven years. He married Susan after his first year in professional football, and Ian was born a year later. A coaching position at the University of Northern Carolina and a warmer climate brought sanity to the family's location. After four years in Belmont, he accepted a coaching job in a tree city named Laurinburg and loved every minute of his career.

Susan Ross Drenn was born in the small community of Leetonia and graduated from the University of Akron. She had met millionaire Edward at the Westgate Mall on a Saturday afternoon. Ten months later, they got married.

Today, they quietly sat watching their only son accept his hard-earned degrees with smiles on their faces. They had a gift for him at the end of the ceremony: a new Rolex wristwatch.

Three days after his graduation, Ian got a job with the Laurinburg Police Department as a police officer and was on six-month probation.

Two hard months later, Susan and Edward Drenn died of COVID-19— just hours apart – leaving behind their only son, Ian Scott Drenn.

For the following three months after his parent's tragic death, Ian would put his heart and soul into training and learning what his duties included. Ian felt alone, and loneliness was nothing to be proud of. Saturdays were his off days, so he would visit the Old Hillside gravesite of his parents to pay respect to them.

"Mom, Dad. I wanted to tell you that Mrs. Locklear and Mrs. Hunt were at your funeral. They brought your favorite flowers and placed them on your grave. Mrs. Hunt told me that if I ever needed to talk to someone, they were available. I didn't know what they meant until now. This being alone is for the birds." He took a step to the next grave, where his father was buried, and said, "Dad, remember that football player you called Sparky who played for the Chicago Bears? Well, he and his wife and six kids showed up for your funeral. That wasn't all. The entire Scotland Flying Scots football squad was there. All of them wore their blue and gold jerseys. I'm a police officer in Laurinburg, but this summer, I'll be working with the Police Athletic League, coaching the little league football teams. I think I'm going to like that." He folded his hands as if in prayer, and added, "I guess that's all for now. I miss you and Mom." He turned to walk away, then turned back. "I almost forgot to tell you. I've been going over to Rockingham. I'm learning how to dance at Tina's Dance Studio. Don't laugh. She says that I'm a natural and that playing quarterback helped me in making moves." He turned away from his parents' gravesite and slowly walked back to his car, tears streaming down his cheeks but feeling better.

Chapter Two

or the next five lonely months, Ian Scott Drenn voluntarily worked the night shift because that was when most crime was being committed. One Saturday, he responded to a domestic disturbance call and immediately drove to the residence. Upon arrival, he knocked on the door and announced that he was a police officer. At that time, the blaring radio was turned off, and that must have been the signal for two men who had come from the north side of the wood house to attack him with shotguns. Ian fell to the ground, bleeding from areas on his abdomen and legs. He was paralyzed to the point that he could hardly move; however, when he was approached by one of the attackers, he found enough strength to pull a backup revolver from his waistline and fired one shot before passing out.

"You never start to live until you've almost died."

Criminologists investigating the situation found fingerprints on the radio and identified the individual as a recently released felon. Blood on the porch, not belonging to Drenn, was identified as belonging to a local blood donor. The third person was not identified, but an all-points bulletin was distributed for the arrest of the two men identified as armed and dangerous. It wouldn't be long before the two men were captured in southern Texas, and they would give up the name of the third accomplice.

Ian Scott Drenn was admitted to the Oban-Scotland Medical Center, where he received treatment until the doctors believed he was fit enough to navigate on his own. They credited the armored vest he was required to wear under his uniform shirt as a lifesaver.

On the following Sunday, he was barely dragging his half-filled green trash bin to the street curb when a very beautiful young lady volunteered to roll the two-wheeled trash bin to the curb for him.

"Thank you," he said with a smile on his face to the beautiful young lady with brown bouncing hair. "I really needed the help."

"If you need help, just telephone me," she offered, then quickly returned to the person waiting for her. They were gone before he knew it.

He returned to the ash-brick house he called home and made his way to the living room, where he turned on the television set and eventually found a comfortable spot on the old sofa. He swore that one day he would get rid of the sofa and buy a new one.

There was a news report on illegal immigration and the knockdown, drag-out street fighting in Democrat-controlled cities. Law enforcement officers were on the menu, and every punk with a desire to degrade a law enforcement officer was going wild. He sympathized with the law enforcement officers.

Just then, he heard a light knock on the front door and hurried over to open it. Standing there, looking at him, was the young lady who had helped him a while ago.

"Hello," he said after opening the storm door and having a smile on his face.

"I forgot to give you my name and telephone number, so I wrote it on this piece of paper," she said as she handed the paper to him.

"Kaitlin Lawrence, 706-7888," he read. "Well, Miss Lawrence, I appreciate your assistance. I really needed your help, and may I call you if I don't need to move a trash bin again?"

She laughed. "We'll see," she said and turned to rejoin her friend.

Drenn gradually closed the glass storm door and let the door to the house stay open to receive the sunlight. Then he watched Kaitlin Lawrence catch up with her friend. Just as he started to leave the doorway, she turned back to see him and waved. He nodded to her with a big smile on his face.

"*Wow*," he said to himself.

Kaitlin asked her friend, "You know what? He asked me if he could call me even if he didn't need help moving the trash container." They laughed.

"What are you going to do, Kaitlin?"

"I don't even know this guy," she replied.

"His name is Drenn. I think. That's the name on the mailbox," her friend said.

"Drenn? I've heard that name before but don't know where?"

"Coach Drenn at Scotland," her friend offered. "You know. The football guy."

"Must be his son because Coach Drenn was a lot older and had a lot of gray hair."

"I'm home, Kaitlin. See you tomorrow morning." Her friend waved to her and walked into her red brick home.

Kaitlin thought of the young Drenn, a smirk appearing on her face. *He's not a bad-looking guy,* she thought.

Ian Scott Drenn was feeling sleepy, but today he had to go for a medical checkup at the Oban-Scotland Medical Center at 2 p.m., and it was time for him to leave. The drive from Purcell Road to the hospital took only a few minutes, but he liked to report in at least fifteen minutes early, so he left the house after turning on the old telephone recording device.

In the alcohol-smelling examination room, his doctor said he was healing as expected and could go back to work in three days. After leaving the doctor's office, he carefully drove to the new Laurinburg Police Station and reported to Chief Darby, telling him he would be back to work on Friday. The Chief said the doctor had called to inform him about it and that he would return to work on the Friday night shift. Drenn leisurely walked out of the station and was glad that he was returning to active duty once more.

He drove his father's teal blue Cadillac west to the US 401 by-pass, then turned south, passing the Walls-Mart Store, and stopping for a barbeque sandwich to eat at home.

After checking the car's fuel gauge, he decided to stop at the gas station and turned onto Blues Farm Road. He noted that gas prices had increased now that Biden had stopped work on the Keystone XL pipeline and was buying fuel from Russia. Our gas money was helping Russia fight the war against the free people of Ukraine. He paid cash for the gas and picked up a lottery form to fill out. For ten dollars, he had one in a hundred million chances of winning some money.

At home, he walked through every room in the house, then sat on the living room sofa with his sandwich and a glass of one percent milk. With the television set programmed to turn off in one hour, he closed his eyes after eating and fell fast asleep. At about 3 a.m., he awoke feeling cold and went to bed fully clothed.

Bright and early Wednesday morning, he dressed in sweat clothes, started a slow jog north on Purcell Road to Blues Farm Road, and then returned. His legs were feeling better, and a warm shower told him not to miss breakfast.

Walking toward his car, he saw gorgeous Kaitlin walking north on Purcell Road and heard her say, "You should be exercising, Mister Drenn!" A big smile was on her face. He turned toward her and replied, "You're late, Miss Lawrence. I've already run two miles, and I'm going for breakfast."

"Likely story, Mister Drenn!" she yelled back to him.

"Be here tomorrow at 6 a.m., and we'll run together Miss Lawrence!" he yelled back to her, then slipped behind the steering wheel.

He smiled to himself. Breakfast that morning was light, and he finished it with a cup of black coffee with just enough cream in it to change its color.

He drove to the police firearms range, presented his identification, and wrapped his ear protection around his neck. The Range Master had just finished running a string of shooters through their firing exercises, and that allowed Drenn to take his place on the range.

"Drenn! Drenn! Go ahead and shoot. You're the last man," the Range Master yelled to him.

Drenn loaded the Beretta Model 92 with fifteen rounds of full metal jacket ammunition, pulled the slide back, and then let it move forward. He fired three rounds at each target from seven feet to thirty yards away.

The Range Master inspected the results of Drenn's shooting. "Drenn, you fired your first round, on every target, to the right of center. That means you are firing too quickly and not aiming. Let's try it again."

"Yes Sir," Drenn replied, continuing to place stickers on his target, covering the bullet holes. This time he took a little longer to fire, but he hit what he was aiming. The Range Master was happy.

"See the difference, Drenn?" The Range Master was holding the target in his hand.

"Yes, Sir." He smiled, checking the hits on the target.

"I thought you were on medical leave, Drenn."

"I return to work on Friday. The second shift, Sir. Just trying to be prepared for what may happen, Sir."

"Good idea. I'll turn in your results to the Chief. See you later, Officer."

After being respectfully dismissed by the Range Master, he walked back to his father's car and drove home. At home that night, he ate a bowl of cold mixed fruit and drank a glass of ice water while watching the eight o'clock movie. Just before going to bed, he wondered if Kaitlin Lawrence would be there at six like they had agreed.

Chapter Three

At exactly five-thirty, the alarm clock shattered Drenn's dreams, and his feet were on the floor five seconds later. After a quick trip to the bathroom, he dressed in a blue sweatsuit with gold-colored letters across the front; he tied the last shoestring at 5:50 a.m. He slowly walked to the mailbox and waited for Kaitlin to arrive. He couldn't believe it. She was walking toward him. He smiled. "Miss Lawrence," he called out. "I'm happy you showed up!"

"You didn't believe I would let your challenge go unanswered, did you?"

"I thought it may be a little early for you," he replied. "But I'm glad you made it. Now do we walk or run?" Again, he challenged her.

"We run, Mister Drenn." Then she read the wording on his sweatshirt. "Police Athletic League. Are you a police officer, Mister Drenn?"

"Yes, Miss Lawrence. For almost two years, I've worked for the Laurinburg Police Department." Thinking she may be against all law enforcement officers, he added, "And I like it." They started walking.

"I thought you would play football or something like that, Mister Drenn."

"I would not turn down a coaching job, but you must have had some experience playing before you get a good-paying job coaching. I am not my father," he explained.

"Do you work, go to school, or what, Miss Lawrence?"

"Have you read a newspaper lately, Mister Drenn?"

"No. I admit I haven't. Why? Are you a reporter?"

"I'm not a newspaper reporter, Mister Drenn. I was a political science and art major in college. For one reason or another, I've been fortunate and became a political cartoonist."

"A political cartoonist. You used both of your majors to create how some people feel and say." He paused. "I would have never guessed it."

"Why, Mister Drenn?"

"Because I have a second degree in recreation and coach little league football."

"In the Police Athletic League," she said. "Do you like working with children?"

"Yes. It develops the mind and body. It's better than having them grow up in a gang or selling drugs on the street corner, Miss Lawrence."

"I can't disagree with that, Mister Drenn."

They walked, talked, and laughed for a mile, then jogged the last mile back. The run ended at Drenn's house, and both were ready to rest. But Kaitlin continued to walk after waving goodbye to Drenn. He smiled and waved back.

After a hot shower, Drenn went back to bed. That night, he reported for duty early and relaxed before going on patrol. His thoughts of Kaitlin were put on the back burner, and his duty took priority over everything else. He drove back home on Saturday morning and was just pulling into the driveway when Kaitlin and her friend were walking north on Purcell Road.

"Hello!" she yelled to him.

He turned to see her coming to the mailbox. "Hello!"

"Are you just going or returning from work?" She asked.

"Just got off. It's been a quiet night."

"That's good, isn't it?"

"Absolutely."

"Nothing happens after dark, does it?"

He was surprised. "Remember the day you helped me with the green trash can? I was recovering from shotgun wounds." Drenn could see the expression on her face change. "I investigated a late-evening domestic disturbance call and was ambushed by two guys with shotguns. That was the reason I needed help."

"Did they catch the bad guys?"

"Yes. They were caught in Texas."

"In Texas? I have to go to a political rally next month in Dallas. What happens if I get shot?"

"If someone shoots you, it will make me really mad. I don't want anything bad to happen to you."

"You care what happens to me?"

"I do." He sounded serious.

"Why?" She acted coy.

"Who will wheel out my green trash can if I get hurt?" He joked, and they laughed.

"You'll never forget that, will you?"

"I like you, Kaitlin. The day you helped me, I was feeling down in the dumps. And when you gave me your name and telephone number, it brightened my day. And each day I see and talk to you, it means a lot to me. I thank you for that." She could tell he was being honest with her.

"You're alone too often, Ian. Maybe you should get out more. Be around people."

"You're absolutely correct, but right now I'm going into the house and going to bed. It's been a long night."

"And I'm going back home. My exercise time is up, and I've got work to do. See you later?"

"I hope so. Goodnight, Kaitlin." He felt exhausted.

She smiled. "Good night, Ian." It was seven thirty in the morning.

For the next three drawn-out months, Drenn would meet Kaitlin going to and returning from work. On a Wednesday morning, Drenn stopped to fill the Cadillac with gasoline, and while there, he filled out the lottery slip and handed ten dollars to the clerk. That morning, he slept without interruption until 5 p.m., and only then did he get up to eat. He was off duty for the next three days, having worked a double shift.

He had caught an individual after a smash-and-grab at Rob's Jewelry Shop, answered a 911 call where someone was attempting to break into a senior's home, and helped a stranded driver when her car ran out of gas. To top off the double shift, he foiled a gas station robbery. All in all, he felt good about himself, and now he was hungry.

After a quick, hot shower, he dressed in casual clothing and was out the glass door a few minutes later. He stopped at the gas station where Blues Farm Road and US 401 South meet to check on his lottery ticket.

When the clerk told him he was a winner, he asked how much he had won. She told him it was around three hundred and sixty million dollars. He told her she was joking, and she said the machine doesn't lie. After comparing the numbers on his ticket to the winning numbers, he became speechless. Then, smiling, he asked, "How would you like to go out on the town tonight and party until dawn?"

She answered, "I would love to, except my husband would object." Then she thanked him, and they laughed.

Using his telephone, he dialed the contact number indicated on the reverse side of the lottery slip and was told to be at a specific location at a specific time. He smiled at the clerk and waved goodbye as he returned home, packed a small overnight bag, and then turned the old Cadillac toward Raleigh. He had forgotten about his hunger, and after driving for about two and a half hours, he found himself in a Raleigh hotel close to the location where he was told to report.

The first thing he had to pay was the taxes, which was about forty percent – about one hundred thirty-six million dollars. Next, he took a "buyout," leaving him with approximately two hundred million dollars for the good. He telephoned his bank and told them what had happened. The

Second Scotland Bank was happy for him and said they would appreciate it if he deposited it with them.

When asked what he was going to do with all of that money, he politely answered that he was hungry and was going to get something to eat. They laughed, and he slowly walked out of the building, believing that someone might stop him and say it was all a joke. But no one did, and he kept walking.

At the bank, he was asked the same question, and he told them he wanted to purchase a new car and some gold bars. The bank manager told him she could help him with both, and he walked out of the bank with a fist full of one-hundred-dollar bills, feeling confident that all was well.

On his way home, he stopped by the gas station and saw the attendant who had told him about the money. To show his appreciation for her honesty, he gave the blond-haired clerk ten thousand dollars in cash. She didn't want to take it, but after a few minutes of insisting, she finally gave in, sobbing as she reluctantly took the money. He felt a little guilty, as he hadn't meant for her to cry.

Chapter Four

It had been many hours since he had eaten, so he turned around and drove to a local restaurant on the US 401 bypass and ate until he couldn't eat anymore. He made a mental note not to run anywhere until his food was fully digested. He was tired and slowly drove home to rest.

Three mornings later, he walked out to the mailbox and observed Kaitlin walking toward him. She smiled when she saw him looking at her.

"Hello," he greeted. "How are you, Kaitlin?"

"Hello, Ian. Are you off work?"

"I worked a double shift and I have three days off. And you?"

"I was published this week by twenty-four newspapers. I feel good."

"You look good. It must be a combination of accomplishment and exercise. Right?"

"It's a combination of living right, Ian."

"I stand corrected. Your trip to Texas must have paid off."

"It did." She stretched her legs, then her arms. "I don't get to exercise when I'm on the road. Have you been busy?"

"Crime never takes a break. I can't figure it out. There are plenty of jobs available in the area. What do we need to stop these people from hurting each other?"

"That's pragmatic, Ian. I don't have an answer, but we have to live one day at a time and do the best we can."

"We've got some illegal people from Mexico working in the area, but they aren't those the ones committing the crimes. What I'm afraid of is when out-of-towners start coming here and creating riots based on politics and race, it's going to cause more problems."

"What we may need is a new President. One that tells D.A.'s to lock up the bad guys and not let them out until they earn it," Kaitlin suggested.

"Yes. Closing the revolving door is a good start, and when a smuggler is caught with fentanyl, he gets the death penalty. Immediately."

"You're a hard man, Ian Drenn," Kaitlin said.

"Just tired of seeing good people hurt and families destroyed. The Chinese Communist Party is allowing deadly drugs to be brought into the United States, and the President wants to play politics. I'm sick of that worthless piece of garbage."

"You're a hard man, Ian Drenn." She repeated. "Are you going jogging this morning?"

"Is it alright if I walk with you?" Kaitlin agreed. And that's what they did. Afterward, they rested on the steps of the hard brick front porch.

"Ian, may I ask you a personal question?"

"That depends on what it is, Kaitlin. Some questions I would rather not answer. But I'll be honest with you. Okay?"

"Fair enough. Question number one: Why are you not married?" Kaitlin wanted to know.

"There was a girl one time I was deeply in love with. She had a singing voice of gold, and I must have watched her movie a half-dozen times," Drenn revealed.

"She was a movie star?" Kaitlin asked while having a smile on her face.

"Yes, she was everything a teenager wanted."

"Well, who was this beautiful movie star?"

"My dad finally told me the movie was nearly fifty years old, and she was now in her senior years. Her name was Lena Born, and she sang Stormy Weather. She was beautiful."

"You're crazy, Ian Scott Drenn." She laughed. "Just plain crazy."

"The person I care about is doing what she trained herself to do, and she enjoys it. I don't want to interrupt her accomplishments. Is that fair enough, Kaitlin?"

"Yes. Question number two: Why is it important for you to be married?"

"Answer number two: I am the last Drenn that I know of in the USA. I want the name of Drenn to survive, and only by being married would the name be saved. Okay?"

"Okay. Question number three. Do you intend to be a police officer for the rest of your life?" She stretched her legs.

"No. My time as a police officer is limited. I know this for sure."

"How do you know that?"

"That question is off limits, Kaitlin."

"I hit a nerve?"

"No. It's just that this is not the time to answer your question. Later. If you don't mind."

"Question: Do I know the person you are interested in?"

"That question is not off limits, but it's difficult to understand what you know."

"Good answer. Do you think you make enough money to support a wife and child?"

"I have enough money to support a wife and child in a manner she is accustomed to and perhaps better. That's really a hard question to answer."

"Is it important that you marry right away?"

"No. I'm a young man. Physically and mentally fit and learning to dance. I can wait."

"Learning to dance?" She laughed. "Your Cadillac is getting old. When do you intend to get a new one?"

"Tomorrow morning, I will leave here and go to the car dealers in Rockingham and purchase a new one. Would you like to go with me?"

"What time are you leaving?"

"About 8:30 a.m. Is that too early for you?"

"I'll be here with a smile on my face."

"Please wear clothing too." They laughed.

"Now may I ask you some personal questions?"

"If they are not too personal."

"Are you married?"

"No." She quickly responded.

"Do you prefer women over men?"

"Boy! You really ask questions! I prefer men."

"If I was hurt in the line of duty, would you help me?"

"Yes."

"Explain the color and model of the automobile you like."

"I don't know that much about cars, but I like cars to reflect the mood I'm in."

"Good answer. What is the oldest car you have ever ridden in?"

"I had a seven-year-old Ford when I was in college. So, the answer would be seven years old."

"I have a car that is sixty-six years old; would you allow me to take you for a ride right now?"

"You're kidding. Sixty-six years old? I would have to see it before giving you an answer, Ian."

"Okay. Follow me." He held the steel wire fence gate open for her when they entered the backyard, and she followed him to a garage where the old car was stored. Opening the locked door, he turned on the lights and allowed her to enter first. What she saw was a vehicle hidden under a large red cloth.

"Wait a minute," he said before removing the protective covering.

She looked at a classic black 1956 Ford Thunderbird with white wall tires and a chrome continental kit. "It's beautiful, but what is it?"

Once he told her what it was and that it ran, she wanted to drive it. "The agreement was that you would take a ride with me, Kaitlin, but I will let you drive it once you get the feel of a small sports car. Okay?"

"Okay. Let's go." Kaitlin got into the T-Bird once Drenn had gently opened the door for her.

After starting the engine, he told her, "Fasten your seat belts." Fumbling for them, she finally found the black belts and fastened herself in.

"The seat belts are a new addition to this model of car. I had them installed for safety reasons as well as a newer engine."

He drove south, then east, on Purcell Road until they got to US 401 South, then he turned to the north. Driving through town drew the attention of many car buffs and the curious. Then he headed to the gas station where Abbotts used to be and turned around, coming to a halt. He slipped out from behind the wheel and walked around to Kaitlin's side of the car. "Ready to drive?" he asked, opening the door.

"Did you see all of those people looking at this car?"

"They were looking at you, Kaitlin. Your smile lit up the way we were going."

"You're full of baloney, Ian." They laughed, and she quickly got behind the steering wheel. Starting it, she slowly placed it into drive. She entered the bypass without any problems and immediately realized that it had a modern turbo-charged engine. She drove past the cemetery, Scotland High School, and then Walls-Mart before turning onto Purcell Road. As they passed by her house, she waved at her mom, who was getting mail from the mailbox. Then she eased the car into Drenn's driveway and parked it under the carport.

"Well, what do you think of my sixty-six-year-old car?" He asked.

"You are not planning on trading it, are you? I want you to keep it." Kaitlin had turned to look into Drenn's face.

"I was going to use Dad's Cadillac for a trade-in, but one of the guys in the department wants to trade it for his pickup truck. So, I'll probably do that. And that creates another problem. How do I get to the dealers in Rockingham and then bring that car back home? Unless we drive the little T-Bird."

"I'll drive the T-Bird back home, Ian."

"You know, I considered that you may want to do just that."

"I had better be getting home, Ian. I've got a lot to think about."

"It's close to noon already, and your mother will want to know what kind of car you were driving."

"Yes, she will. I'll see you tomorrow morning, wearing clothes." They laughed.

"Would you like for me to take you home in the T-Bird?"

"No. I need to think while I'm walking, Ian."

"I understand. Take care." He watched as she walked down Purcell Road.

Kaitlin thought about what Ian had told her when she was questioning him. The one question she wondered about was about him being a police officer. How did he know he would not be a police officer for long? She made a mental note to follow up on that question. She opened the front door to her home when she arrived.

Chapter Five

alking into the kitchen, she saw her mother making lunch and retrieved a cold soda from the refrigerator before taking a seat at the table.

"Was that you waving at me from that little car, Kaitlin?" Her mother wanted to know.

"Yes, Mom." She appeared to be happy.

"Who was with you, D?" Her mother sat a bowl of chicken noodle soup and a grilled cheese sandwich in front of her.

"That was Ian Scott Drenn, Mom. He's interested in me but doesn't come out to say it in plain language."

Her mother sat across from her.

"He said, in so many words, that he wants me to excel in my work but doesn't tell me what happens afterward. Isn't that strange, Mom?"

"And how did you come to drive the little car?" They ate while they talked.

"It's a 1956 T-Bird. We drove through town, and everyone was looking at us. He said the smile on my face lit up the way we were going."

"Hmmm, sounds like he's a romantic, Dear. Do you like him?"

"Yes, I do like him. I like him a lot. But there appears to be something going on in his mind that I just can't understand."

"What did the young man say D?"

"It was something about not being a police officer for long."

"Maybe he has found a better-paying job. You know police officers don't make a lot of money, and people are protesting against the police, and the Socialist-Democrats want to defund the departments."

"That could be it." She put on a happy face and told her mother, "Tomorrow, I'm going with him to Rockingham to purchase a new car."

"A new car? You just told me he was not going to be a police officer for very long, and now he's buying a new car? Is he a millionaire police officer?"

"I wish." She paused. "He may not be a millionaire, Mom, but he's one of the nicest guys I've ever met." She laughed.

"What is it?" her mother asked.

"He told me he's taking dance lessons at Tina's Dance Studio in Rockingham." Again, they laughed.

"Well, maybe he doesn't know how to dance. But then again. Maybe what you could do is go to the studio and tell Tina you want to dance with Ian. That way, you two will know each other's steps."

"Brilliant idea. I'll do just that. Now I think I've got an idea I want to put on paper." Kaitlin got up from the table, rinsed her bowl and spoon, and then put them in the dishwasher. "See you later, Mom."

"Yes, dear," her mother replied while sitting at the table. "*Mothers can help their daughters once in a while*," she thought.

That night at the dinner, Kaitlin's father mentioned the little car, and Kaitlin responded. "It's a 1956 Ford T-Bird, Dad."

"Ahh, a T-Bird. A thunderbird, Honey?"

"That's what he called it, and it drives great."

"And what does this young man do for a living?"

"He's a Laurinburg Police Officer, Dad, and I like him a lot."

"And where does he live, Honey?"

"Just down the street, Dad. He's the son of Coach Drenn."

"The Scotland Flying Scots, Coach Drenn?"

"Yes, Dad."

"The Drenns are good people. Good Republicans. Excellent football coach. Few are left alive in the United States, though."

"Where are they originally from, Dad?"

"Most of the Drenn families are from Old England, Scotland, and Ireland but settled in eastern Pennsylvania before the Revolutionary War.

"And just how do you know this, Dad?"

"It's your father's hobby, D," her mother interrupted. "He's been into the heritage thing for years."

"I didn't know that about you, Dad."

"Did you know your father drove an old green pickup truck when he was going to college? I thought he was a farmer until he told me he was going into pre-med, and that changed everything. When you came along, he was still driving the same old green pickup truck. Then, for one reason or another, he bought a car."

"That was when Mister Catton paid his doctor's bill." He laughed. "I remember that day. You wanted a blue Pontiac, and I wanted a white one. We settled on a beautiful gold-colored Lincoln."

"The Pontiac was beautiful too," Mom added.

"I know when I'm beaten. The Pontiac was beautiful too.." He waited for his wife to say something. "You know, Mrs. Lawrence, I'm off duty for the next four days. How would you like to go to the beach?"

"You know, Mister Lawrence, I have our clothes already packed. Do you want to leave now?"

"Yes, Dear." Kaitlin's parents excused themselves from the table.

It was nearly six-thirty before they departed Laurinburg, heading for the coast. Kaitlin picked up the house telephone and dialed Ian's number.

"Drenn residence," he answered.

"Hello, Drenn. This is Kaitlin."

"Hi. What's going on?"

"Mom and Dad just left for the coast, and I'm all alone. I was thinking of you, so I telephoned."

"Well, I'm glad you did. I was thinking of you, and I'm all alone. But if we were together, we wouldn't be alone."

"I know what you're thinking, and I know what would happen if we were together. So, what are you doing?" she asked.

"Well, let's see. After you left, I showered, shaved, and dressed in my best green, yellow, and blue pajamas to sit on the sofa and watch a baseball game. Oh yes, I popped some corn, and the house smells good. So here I am. All alone and missing you."

"Your sob story breaks my heart, Ian Scott Drenn. And if I come over there, you and I know what will happen and how our relationship will change. I like you at a safe distance," Kaitlin told him, and she could hear him laugh.

"You're right. I don't want to risk what we have, Kaitlin."

"Give me an idea for a cartoon, Ian. This way, I can stay busy tonight."

"Okay. How about one on spying balloons."

"Keep going," she urged.

"The President of the USA aided and abetted the Chinese Communist Party to cause the spying of US missile bases by electronic data, relaying balloons to weaken our armed forces defensive posture."

"That's something to think about, and it's a good idea. Got another?"

"Sure. How about aiding and abetting the Russian Communist Party by closing the Keystone XL pipeline, causing the US to purchase fuel from Russia so they may continue their war against Ukraine using taxpayer money? How about that?"

"Good. Give me another."

"Aiding and abetting the Chinese Communist Party by selling them fuel from the Strategic Petroleum Reserve weakens our US armed forces."

"Okay, one more."

"Biden gives Iran fifteen billion dollars to halt their nuclear program. Iran uses the money to support Russia's war in Ukraine. In essence, our tax money is supporting Russia's war while the US supports Ukraine fighting Russia."

"That's enough for a while. I'm glad you know something about what's going on in the world. Right now, I'm off to my studio to get you off my mind. See you in the morning, Ian."

"Goodnight, Kaitlin."

"Goodnight, Ian," she said, slowly hanging up the house telephone.

Ian Scott Drenn thought for a second and smiled to himself. He hung up the telephone and reached for the bowl of buttered popcorn.

Chapter Six

n Saturday morning, he was up bright and early and the first thing that came to his mind was to telephone Kaitlin. "Hello."

"Kaitlin, how about breakfast at Biscuitvalley this morning, then we can leave from there?"

"Sounds good to me."

"I'm on the way to your house," he told her.

"I'm walking out the front door, Ian."

He stopped in front of the Lawrences' white brick house and opened the car door for her. After settling in the car, they made their way to get breakfast. "Did you get any sleep?"

"Yes, and I did a month's work last night after your suggestions."

"A month's work. Wow! Hungry?"

"Yes. Starved."

"Biscuitvalley okay?" He asked.

"Breakfast platter with bacon, grits, no butter. Orange juice." She ordered, showing she had been there before.

"Got it." He acknowledged her order and, in twenty minutes, doubled the same order to the Order Taker. Kaitlin was waiting for him at a table. "You know, this morning we are going to make some car salesman's dream come true."

"This will be our first breakfast together, Ian."

"I hope there will be many more, Kaitlin, and when the time is right, it will be at our own table."

"I have a confession to make, and you may not like it," Kaitlin told him.

"You don't know how to cook," he said, trying to be funny.

"How did you know?" She was serious.

"You're kidding," he said.

"I'm not a good cook, but as long as I have a microwave, we won't go hungry." They laughed.

"Let's get out of here." They walked outside to see a half dozen people inspecting the Ford Thunderbird.

"What year is it?" Someone asked.

"It's a 1956 Ford Thunderbird," Kaitlin answered. She saw Ian smile and nod to her.

"How fast will it go?" Another person asked.

"It's got a turbocharged engine and tops out at about a hundred and seventy, but not using these tires and gasoline." She smiled and got behind the wheel. A few minutes later, they were on US 74, driving toward the west. They were quiet until Kaitlin broke the silence with a question when they were approaching Laurinburg city limits.

"Did I say all the right things?"

"Absolutely, Honey. I mean Kaitlin. Put the metal to the pedal."

She slowed down going through Hamlet and took the back entrance to the Cadillac dealers in Rockingham. Kaitlin came to a stop in front of a shiny, new, dark green four-door Cadillac. She slowly turned her head toward Ian and smiled. "This one, Ian."

"Dark green?" *It was the color of the green beret that Special Forces operators wear,* he thought.

"Dark green, Ian."

"Are you sure?" he asked, looking at the car.

"Yep." She could see a salesman walking toward them and waiting for him to say something.

The salesman circled the T-Bird and said, "Nice wheels. Do you want to trade it?"

"No thanks. I'm looking to buy a new Cadillac," she told him.

"We've got a fair collection of used Cadillacs and a few new ones. Have you seen anything you like?"

"How much is that blue one over there at the back entrance?"

"That one is four years old but is in excellent condition. We can make you a good deal," he offered.

"How about the dark green one?" She asked and pointed to the car they were parked in front of.

"It's new. Just got it in last week. It is dark green, but it's called evergreen. You know. Like the trees. I can make you a good trade."

"Let's talk numbers. Our bank is just across the street. Maybe we can come to a deal," Kaitlin said. The salesman led the way inside, and Kaitlin asked Ian how she was doing. "You're buying it for me. Remember that."

The salesman wanted the T-Bird, but Kaitlin didn't want to give it up. Finally, they settled on a price, and she turned to Ian and told him to get the money. Ian left her with the new, evergreen-colored Cadillac and drove across the street to the Second Scotland Bank. There, he obtained an official check for the exact amount Kaitlin and the salesman had agreed on and drove back to the car dealership to Kaitlin. There he gave the check to Kaitlin, who gave it to the salesman. The salesman was surprised and did all he could for her. Eventually, Ian drove the new car home while Kaitlin followed him in the classic black T-Bird.

He parked the new car under the carport and was met at the rear of the car by an excited Kaitlin. They hugged each other and laughed, jumping up and down like a couple of clowns. When they stopped, Drenn kissed her, and she kissed him back. The kiss changed everything. Something was different about how they were together after that moment.

"You were great, Kaitlin," Ian said to her with a big smile on his face and still holding her.

"I thought I was going to laugh when I gave him that check and saw the look on his face. We made his day, and he'll talk about this for years!"

"You're a great actress, and I just had to go along with whatever was happening," he said.

"I was a little worried when you left me there, but then when you returned so quickly, I was okay." She told him while holding onto his waist.

"I left you there to make him think you were in charge of me, and he went along with that." He could feel her body relax in his arms.

"Do you like holding me in your arms?" she asked while still holding on to him.

"Yes. We should do this more. I like holding on to you."

"I would like for you to hold me, Ian. And you are being very careful not to drive a wedge between us. Why is that?"

"I'm a police officer, Kaitlin. I won't always be, but I don't want to make any mistakes with you," he explained.

"You've made a mistake. With whom? Do I know her?"

"It's not a her. I walked into a domestic disturbance and got shot by two guys with shotguns. For some reason, that has transformed itself into our relationship. I don't want to make a mistake with you."

"I understand, Ian." She thought for a second. "You have been a gentleman with me, and I like being treated with respect. Now let's take a ride in your new dark green Cadillac, and you can buy me lunch."

"Then we should take his thing out to I-95 and see what it will do. Are you game?" he asked.

"I'm game, and I'm hungry."

"Where to?"

"That place on US 401 bypass."

"Okay," he said, holding the door to the new, evergreen-colored Cadillac open for her. She smiled and got in.

After lunch, he drove east toward US 74, then south toward South Carolina.

"You better slow down, Ian," Kaitlin warned. "You're doing over eighty-five miles per hour." She could feel the car starting to slow down.

"This thing will really go, and you'll never even feel it." He praised the car's capability.

"You've got to be careful, Ian. Learn how to handle it," she advised.

"You're right." He drove on to the Just South of the Border Motel and turned around, heading north to Rowland, then on to US 501, and then asked Kaitlin if she wanted to drive. She cheerfully replied that it would be nice if he let her drive the new car. And she did – all the way back to his house on Purcell Road.

"Well, what do you think of it?"

"It's like driving a cloud. Smooth. Easy on the road. But there are so many electronics in here. I would almost bet there's a microwave oven hidden somewhere in it," she said to him.

Chapter Seven

"May I ask you a personal question, Ian?"

"As long as it's not too personal. Go ahead."

"Do you love me?" She was serious.

He thought about a good answer and said, "If I say yes, that would be too simple of an answer. If I say no, that would be a lie. May I ask you the same question?"

"Good answer. How do you feel about me going everywhere to gather material for my job?"

"That's a good question, Kaitlin. I think that if we were married, I would have a different feeling toward you than I would have not been married to you. If we were married, I would want to go with you at certain times, depending on what I was engaged in. But since we are not married, I leave you to do what you have to or must do to accomplish your goals."

"Good answer. You have faith in me to do what I must do and that I will not do anything to dishonor our relationship."

"Yes."

"Thank you, Ian, and I have deep feelings for you too."

"Thank you for your honesty. Too many people in the White House have forgotten what the words honor and respect mean. To me, they are a way of life."

"What do you mean when you say you will not be a police officer much longer?"

"I have thought about getting my bachelor's degree, but I want to complete three years as a police officer first," he responded.

"Then go back to law enforcement?"

"I don't think so. I want to complete three years as a police officer before changing. That's important to me."

"Why is it important to you?"

"Because I would have completed my duty to the community. You could say it was a service to the nation. Like being in the Army."

"That's a very unusual approach to serving your country."

"It's unusual because the anti-Americans are trying to tear down the security offered by the police. They are doing their best to destroy rather than build. They are doing their best to divide our people, like having a war between races. I've heard the President of the United States, Joe Biden, say that white people are a danger to this country. I've heard him call loyal citizens of this country names despicable and deserving of hatred and contempt. I never heard President Trump say things like that about our people."

"I know what you mean, Ian."

"You know we're sitting in a new car talking about solving the nation's problems when we should be holding hands, being in each other's arms, or—" He was abruptly interrupted.

"That's far enough, Ian."

"I was just going to say, trying to see if you can cook without a microwave." He laughed.

"What do you say we get out of your new evergreen Cadillac? I need to use your bathroom."

"Let's go." They slipped out of the car and entered the house. Kaitlin promptly moved to the bathroom after Ian pointed the way, and he tried to relax on the sofa.

When Kaitlin joined him, she asked, "What's on your agenda for tomorrow?" Then she sat on the old sofa and tried to be comfortable.

"I don't have anything on my agenda. What would you like to do?"

"What do you say that we just play it by ear? Take a drive in the T-Bird, and you can feed me."

"Sounds okay to me. What time should I pick you up?"

"Nine o'clock okay? But right now, I've got to get home. Mom will be telephoning me soon to see if I'm okay, and I don't want to worry her."

"Would you like to drive the T-Bird or the new evergreen Cadillac?"

"Let's take the T-Bird."

"Let's get out of here." A few minutes later, Ian drove Kaitlin home and headed back to the house.

The next morning, he picked Kaitlin up at her house and drove to a local restaurant for breakfast. "Kaitlin, let me ask you something. I've always understood that before two people get married, they are normally engaged. Is that correct?"

"Correct."

"Do you enjoy your time with me?"

"Yes." She thought for a brief moment. "Are you asking me if I will marry you?"

"I was thinking that if you wanted to continue your career while being married to me would not be the best for you. But being engaged and not setting a date to be married would allow you to pursue your dreams. Does that make sense?"

She smiled. "Yes, Ian, that makes a lot of sense. Just a couple of things you should understand. One, you have never told me you love me, and two, you've never asked me to marry you."

"You know, you're right. I like you. I like being around you. I like talking with you, and I like your brilliant sense of humor. I like the warm feeling of you. I like what you do, but is that love?"

"You have a handle on it, Ian. I like everything about you except your job. Being the wife of a police officer doesn't offer the security a woman is looking for. In this day and age, it's open season on law enforcement officers, and it's not going to get any better until we have a change of Presidents and Democratic Governors running states."

"Then if I said I could offer you security, would that be something you'd consider?"

"Absolutely. Bringing up a child alone means putting your own dreams aside and is a very hard thing to do."

"I agree. Ready to leave."

"Yes." They stepped outside to find about four or five boys checking out the T-Bird.

"How fast will it go?" One little boy asked.

"She'll do about one hundred and seventy miles per hour on a good day," Kaitlin answered, enjoying the attention.

"Can you give us a ride in it?" a ten-year-old boy asked.

"Not today, boys. I'm taking this policeman for a ride." She turned her head toward Ian.

"Can I drive it just a little bit, Honey?" he pleaded.

"He called her Honey!" one of the boys yelled out, and they laughed.

"Not today, Dear," she responded.

"She called him Dear!" A boy yelled, and they laughed even more.

She cautiously drove out of the parking area, and both of them started laughing once they were clear of the boys.

"You know we were young once." Ian asserted.

She turned north out of Biscuitvalley and then west on US 74 through Hamlet, Rockingham, Wadesboro, and Monroe. She kept within the speed limit and had a smile on her face the whole time. Finally, she turned into a large parking lot. "I've been driving for two hours, and I'm tired."

"Only two hours? I'll bet you enjoyed every minute of it."

"I did." She appeared exhausted. "One thing I learned the hard way was that this is not a vehicle I would want to drive a long-distance in. Like on a vacation," she said to Ian, who was getting out of the T-Bird. She watched him stretch his shoulders and legs.

"You're absolutely correct, but I've been thinking that perhaps if the tires were changed or maybe a different set of shock absorbers were installed, it may be easier on the back."

"That's an idea. It's no Cadillac." She laughed. "Oh, I almost forgot to tell you. I received a message yesterday from my employer. He wants me to cover the political rally for De Sartor in Cedar Rapids, Iowa, next week. Are you okay with this?"

"Not really, but this is what you do. You know there are some bad people out there. Would you use some tear gas if I gave it to you? I'll show you how to use it just in case you get into trouble."

"You want to protect me?"

"Yes, you know I can't be there with you."

"I've never had any problems before."

"The United States is in major trouble with Biden the Boss, our country's a loss, and it's not going to get any better until he's gone for good."

"I agree," Kaitlin responded.

"Okay. Get in the car. It's time for me to put the pedal to the metal."

They arrived back at Ian's house and pulled the car directly into the secured garage. He helped Kaitlin out of the car and went into his home. There, he brought out a small can of tear gas and had her watch him use it in the backyard. "Now you point it and press down on the top of the can." She did, and a stream of liquid tear gas spurted out almost twelve feet. "Never shoot this stuff in the wind; otherwise, you will be the victim and start crying."

"Okay, Ian," she said. "Better get me home now, or you will never get any sleep."

"Cadillac, Honey."

"Yes, Dear." They laughed.

Chapter Eight

That night, Ian readily reported for duty a little early just to get the feel of going back to work. The night staff stood for inspection and was briefed on potential trouble spots. All was quiet in the city of Laurinburg. For the next couple of months, the weather began to change, football season was coming to an end, and Kaitlin was steadily working. Homer Williams was trying his best to be elected to the US House of Representatives.

Kaitlin had invented the saying, "A Vote for Homer was a Home run for America." Her employer liked it and gave her a small raise. She loved the work she was doing, and Ian often praised her for her accomplishments.

Late one cold evening, Drenn responded to a domestic disturbance call. Remembering what had happened to him earlier in his work, he turned on his camera and opened the recording mic. He knocked loudly on the door, and a man soon opened it. "Would you please turn down the radio or television so we can talk?" he politely asked, but the man refused to turn down the volume on the television. "Can you hear me?" he asked, using sign language.

"I can f… hear you!" the man retorted. "What the f… is the trouble?" he yelled at Ian.

"We have received complaints about the noise coming from your house," Ian explained.

"Noise? What f... noise?" The man was belligerent and used foul language.

"Yea, what noise!" A large-sized woman standing beside him asked. "We ain't making a G.. d.. noise!"

"We received complaints about the noise coming from this house," he repeated. "And would appreciate it if you would turn the television down," he politely explained.

The woman closed in on his position and yelled at him, "We ain't turning a f... television set down for you or anyone else!" She yelled just a few inches from his face.

He stepped back and wiped her saliva from his face with his handkerchief. Then he put it in a small plastic bag, placed it inside his waistband, and watched as she circled him.

"Lady, stay away from me," he warned her.

"She ain't no f... lady, you a.. hole!" The man yelled at him and started to close in on him.

"Stay back, Sir!" Ian warned.

"You're hurting me!" the big woman suddenly screamed, but Ian was nowhere near her. "You're hurting me!" she screamed again while backing away from the man who was also backing away from him.

Then Ian turned to see a boy, about twelve years old, standing in a doorway and armed with a large caliber revolver. The revolver was aimed at Ian.

"He hurt me! He hurt me! He hurt me!" she abruptly cried, rubbing her arm.

The boy cocked the revolver with two hands.

Ian slowly removed his Beretta from its holster and softly spoke to the boy as if giving him a lesson on firearms. "This is a Beretta 9-millimeter pistol, and it has a blue finish and a five-inch barrel. As you can see, the safety is off, but I see the safety on your revolver is still on." He was trying to confuse the boy, then looked into a wall mirror and saw the man and woman nodding their heads up and down and signaling to the boy to shoot him. "Now if you look on that side of your revolver," Ian pointed to the right side, "you can see the safety and remove it before firing."

The boy turned the revolver to one side, and Ian attempted to knock it out of his hand but failed. The boy pulled the trigger and dropped the revolver.

Ian was shot in the right leg, six inches below the knee, and he fell to the floor. The woman grabbed the revolver and pointed it at him. Ian immediately fired two shots. The man had quickly disappeared.

By the time the ambulance and police got there, Ian was in major pain. He never remembered when the ambulance arrived or was questioned by his fellow officers, but he did give them the small plastic bag with the handkerchief and the woman's saliva on it. He awoke in the hospital with his right leg in a cast. Someone was using a cold, wet cloth to wipe his right arm. He slowly opened his eyes to see that it was a nurse's aide. His mouth felt cotton dry, and he had a slight headache.

"You're awake," she declared and then stopped washing him. "I'll get a nurse," she said and departed. A few moments later, a nurse arrived.

"How do you feel?" She wanted to know and stuck a thermometer in his mouth. He grunted.

A few minutes later, a familiar-looking doctor told him about the wound. "The bullet pierced the lower fibula and tore out about a half inch of bone. We replaced the bone, and you shouldn't have a limp," he was told in medical terminology, and he assumed this was to make him understand his recovery was going to take weeks.

"Do you have someone who can look after you?" the doctor asked.

"No. I'm alone."

"Alright. I'll move you to rehab in a couple of days."

"Thanks." Three days later, he was moved to rehabilitation, and two weeks later, he started a system of exercises that was designed to make him walk again. Even playing football, he had never felt the pain he felt working out. Then, the overworked Chief of Police visited him.

"How are you, Drenn?" Chief Darby sat in one of the two chairs in his room.

"He was twelve years old, Chief, and even with a revolver pointed at me, I couldn't shoot him," he explained.

"A couple of the local citizens gave us a description of the man and the boy. We have them both in jail."

"I watched the man and the woman, in a mirror, urge this boy to shoot me."

"We've got enough evidence from your body camera and the open mic to put them away for a long time, Drenn."

"That's good. Am I going to stay a police officer?"

"That's the bad news, Drenn. You've been an excellent officer, but the doctor's report says no. I've cleaned out your locker and put everything you owned in your car trunk. But while I am here, I'll present you with your second Scotland Heart Medal for the wounds you've received and another Police Commendation Medal for your actions in solving this case. And you'll receive a small medical retirement based on your number of years of service, Drenn. It won't be much, but it will buy you a box of ammo."

"Thanks, Chief."

"You're a young man, Drenn. Take my advice and go back to college. Learn something, but don't kick any footballs or backsides." He was edging toward the exit.

"Thanks for coming, Chief."

Chief Darby saluted him as he departed, and Drenn felt a little better. He looked at the medals. All he had to do now was get out of this place. The food was excellent, but what he needed to see was some nice friendly faces.

The following Wednesday's cold afternoon, Kaitlin returned from Iowa and was happy to see him. He got a kiss on the cheek but felt it was a kiss from a distance.

"How are you feeling, Ian?" She didn't wait for an answer. "I've missed you."

"Okay. I'll be out of here in four or five weeks, and the Chief gave me my walking papers today. A medical retirement. How are you?"

She sat in the same chair the Chief of Police had sat in. "I've been busy working for the past two weeks. I didn't even know you had been injured until I went to the gas station and a blond clerk told me you had been shot. I guess you couldn't call me." She stopped talking. "What are you going to do?"

"Laying in here thinking about the future has been a little rough. My thoughts are mixed up. I can't give you an honest, definite answer. But I know my degrees are worthless, so learning something new is on my agenda. Maybe go back to school, but the trouble is I don't know what field I want to go into."

"That sounds positive, Ian. Do you have enough money to support yourself?"

"Money? Well, I thought you would support me. That's a joke, Kaitlin. I have enough money to do what I want to do."

"Are you sure? I've got some money stashed away; you can have it." She believed all he had was what he earned as a police officer and had saved.

"Thank you, but I really don't worry about money." He didn't tell her he won the lottery.

"Stop kidding around. I'm serious."

"Kaitlin, Honey, I don't worry about money because I don't have to. Understand?"

"I don't understand. You say you don't have to worry about money, but you're out of work now, and I care about you."

"I'm glad you care for me, Kaitlin. But I'll tell you again. I don't have to worry about money." He looked into her eyes and saw tears forming. He took her hand in his and gently lifted her chin. "Listen to me, Kaitlin. I care for you very much, and I don't want you to cry for me. I have enough money that will last me for a very long time."

"I don't know when to take you seriously. Are you kidding me?" She still didn't understand what he was telling her.

"I don't know how to prove to you that I'm financially stable. Laying in this bed has its limitations, Kaitlin. Tell me about your work."

"You're trying to change the subject, Ian. I'm smart enough to realize that."

"I don't want to have to prove to you that I'm financially stable. I want you to love me for what I am."

"I want to know if you can support a wife and child, Ian. It's called family security."

Chapter Nine

Supper that evening was at 6 p.m., and the entire family of three sat around the table.

Mrs. Lawrence had ensured the meal was hot and on time when her husband got home from the hospital.

It was Kaitlin who broke the silence at the table. "Dad, did you work on Ian's leg injury?"

"Yes, Dear." Her father put down his knife and fork to listen to his daughter.

"Is he going to walk again?" She played in her salad with a fork.

"He's walking now, Dear. He was sent to rehab to learn to walk all over, and from what I understand, he's doing fine."

"Will he walk with a limp?"

"No, I don't think so. If you are interested in his activities, Dear, why not visit rehab during the non-visiting hours."

"And how do I do that?"

"Tell them who you are and why you are there for me."

"I'll call rehab and tell them you're coming. Is that okay?"

"Thanks, Dad."

"Can I eat supper now?" Mr. Lawrence picked up his fork.

"Yes, Dad." Kaitlin gave him a thank you smile.

"Why the interest in this guy?" Her father asked while putting some salad dressing on his vegetable salad.

"I like him a lot, Dad, and I offered to help him financially, but he wouldn't take it."

"I can understand his feelings. You see, Mister Drenn is financially secure, having won three hundred and forty million dollars playing the lottery," her mother informed her. "After forty percent taxes, he probably brought home two hundred million," her mother added. "And if he was smart, he purchased at least fifty million dollars' worth of gold. Like your father does, Dear."

Kaitlin was stunned. "He didn't tell me that, Dad, Mom. He just repeatedly said that he was financially secure."

"He didn't tell you because he wanted you to love him for him and not for the money," her mother said.

"That makes sense, Mom."

"Just don't tell him you know about the money and take him for who he is," her mother suggested. "Otherwise, you'll lose him."

"Now I can understand how he paid cash for his new car," Kaitlin admitted.

"How's your supper, Dear?"

"It couldn't be better, Mom." Kaitlin took another bite of her food, and then asked her mother, "Did you have this many problems with Dad?"

Her father's ears perked up as he waited for his wife to answer.

"No, Dear. Your father and I met before he went into pre-med. I knew what he wanted out of life, and I was willing to wait until he was in the last phase of his training."

"Mom, it seems like history is repeating itself. Ian wants me to succeed in my job and is willing to wait for a while. But I don't know how long he will wait."

"That's a problem that only you can solve, Dear. So let me ask you this: Does the money he has made, make a difference in your relationship with Ian?" her mother asked.

"Yes. It offers security, and security is important to me," Kaitlin answered.

"If you didn't know about the money, would that make a difference?"

"Yes, because I want to know if we, as a family, can survive," she answered.

"Do you love him for what he is or what he can give you?"

"I love him for what he is and his ability to provide security for us as a family."

"Are you willing to give up your career to have a family with him?"

"Yes, Mom. The stuff of what I have to go through isn't worth losing him."

"Then, my Dear, marry the guy before you lose him," Kaitlin's mom advised.

"What your mother isn't telling you is that she gave up her career to marry me, Kaitlin," her father revealed. "Your mother had a brilliant career in newspaper advertising art."

"I didn't know that about you, Mom." She saw her mother smile.

"I wasn't that good, Dear," her mother admitted.

"Yes, you were," her father acclaimed.

That evening, Kaitlin stopped by the gas station, bought Ian's favorite snack, then drove to the rehab center.

Walking to Ian's room, she knocked on the door and waited for an answer before she entered.

He was sitting up in the hospital bed and exercising his injured leg and immediately stopped when he saw her. "Hello, Kaitlin." He was especially happy to see her.

"I brought you something you might like, Ian," she said as she handed him two small containers of strawberry ice cream. They were still in a plastic bag with the name of Ian's favorite gas station printed on it.

He smiled after looking inside the bag. "Aaah, ice cream. You know the way to my heart!"

"If that's the way to your heart, I'll bring you gallons of strawberry ice cream every day," Kaitlin jokes.

"Thank you, and you already have my heart."

"Is there anything I can do for you? Do you need anything?"

"Yes, there is. I need a couple of things. First, my car is parked in the police station parking lot. Will you please have someone bring it to me? And park it outside this building. That way, I will have transportation home. Second. I have been without underwear for almost four weeks now." He could see Kaitlin cover her mouth, trying to hide her laughter. "Would you go to my house and into my bedroom and get me some clothes to wear? Underwear, a sweatshirt, trousers, socks, and tennis shoes. Here, I've got it all written down on paper. Please." He handed her the slip of notebook paper. He could see the smile on her face. "Don't laugh."

But she did. Holding out her hand, she waited for him to place the keys into it.

He gently placed the keys to his car and house into her hand and had to laugh along with her.

"Anything else?"

"Yes. A kiss." He pointed a finger to where he wanted her to kiss him.

She removed herself from the soft, wooden chair and walked to him, then bent over at the waist, and they kissed.

"I want that more often, Kaitlin. I like it."

"I like it too. Now eat your ice cream and get back to where we can go dancing." She backed out of the room and waved goodbye to him. She saw him smile at her before closing the door.

She slowly drove home that night, making plans to accomplish all that Ian wanted. Her mother would drive her car while she drove Ian's Cadillac. She would get his blue sweatshirt and pants with no problems in the morning. That night, sleep came easily.

Peeking out of her bedroom window, she saw a light coating of frost on the ground and rooftops. She made a mental note to include a medium-weight jacket for Ian.

In the kitchen, she sipped on a cup of hot tea with a squeeze of lemon in it. "Ready, Mom?"

"Let's go." Mrs. Lawrence was slipping into her lightweight, tan-colored car coat.

They entered Ian's warm house and went straight to his bedroom. His shorts were rolled and placed on the right-hand side of a dresser drawer, and his t-shirts were neatly folded and double stacked about six shirts high on the left side of the same drawer. Socks were divided into white on the left and colored on the right in another drawer.

Her mother found a small black nylon suitcase and laid it on his bed. The things were packed in a short time, and they locked the side door behind them. The next stop was the police parking lot.

Her mother followed her to the rehabilitation center, immediately removing the suitcase and handing it to Kaitlin.

It was exercise time for Ian, so he never observed Kaitlin bring the suitcase in and leave his keys under it. She went back out the door and into her mother's car. "Mission accomplished, Mom. I'll buy you breakfast at Biscuitvalley."

"You're buying?" she asked with a smile on her face.

"Yep."

"I'm eating," her mother jokingly responded.

Later that cool afternoon, Kaitlin Lawrence received a telephone call from her boss, wanting her to cover the political rally in Richmond, Virginia. She accepted the assignment.

Visiting hours at the McDonald Rehabilitation Center started just after supper hours, and she was lightly knocking on Ian's room door a moment later.

"Did I pack enough clothes for you?" She wanted to be sure.

"You got everything I needed, Kaitlin."

"Mom helped me, and your car is parked close to the entrance. Now I'm going to be gone, starting early on Thursday morning. I've got an assignment in Richmond, Virginia, so I'll be back sometime on Sunday morning. I can pick up your dirty clothes then, Ian."

"Thanks, Kaitlin. I really appreciate this." He thought for a moment. "This guy, what's his name? Is he still trying to get elected?"

"Yes. His name is Homer Williams. A Vote for Homer Williams is a Home Run for America. Remember?"

"Now, how about this? Homer Williams is a Home Run for the Voter," Ian offered.

"You're getting the idea, Ian. May I use it?" She removed a small red notebook and pen from her pocket and wrote in it, then placed them back in her coat pocket.

"Of course," he said, "whatever you do, be proud of it. Give it all you've got. Be the best."

"Thank you but let me say this. Being at one of the rallies is like being in jail. You can't move or say what you really feel. If I did, I would be out of a job. Homer Williams is no one I would vote for."

"What's wrong with Homer Williams?"

"He has some idea that being a member of the US House of Representatives is like a position on God's personal staff and that whatever he does or says is the truth. In reality, I wouldn't let him shine my shoes. But I like the money," she admitted.

"You compromise your own beliefs to make him look good?"

"I do."

"Then why don't you run for an elected office?" Ian asked. "I think you would make a good Senator or maybe even Governor."

"Thank you, but housewife and mother sound better."

"Kaitlin?"

"Yes."

"I think it's about time I put an engagement ring on your finger. Would you accept it with my love?"

"Ian, I would be proud to be engaged to you."

"I don't know when I will escape from here, but I do have a ring to put on your finger in my dresser drawer."

She smiled, waiting for him to tell her where the ring was.

"And you want me to return to your house and obtain the ring and bring it to you so you can place it on my finger?"

"And clean out the mailbox, please."

"How do you know my ring's size?"

"That's top secret, Kaitlin."

"Okay, tell me again where to find the ring."

"In my bedroom, on the dresser on the north side of the room, a second drawer from the top, on the right side of the drawer, in a dark red velvet bag marked Seagram's VO, there is a small blue box with the ring in it. Please bring the bag with the ring box in it to me."

"Got it. See you in an hour. Bye."

Less than an hour later, Kaitlin reentered the Rehabilitation Center and softly knocked on the wooden door to Ian's room. Ian told her to come in, and she was surprised to see her mother and father sitting in the only two chairs in the room.

"Mom, Dad, what are you doing here?"

"It's visiting hours, Dear," her mother answered with a smile on her face.

Kaitlin handed the bag and his mail to Ian and watched as he removed the small box from the red velvet bag.

"Sit on the bed, Kaitlin," he directed. Drenn stood up, then kneeled down on one knee. He removed the ring from the box and said, "Kaitlin, with this ring, I ask you to marry me. Date TBA." Everyone in the room laughed.

"Ian Scott Drenn. Of course, I will marry you," she said, and with a big smile on her face, echoed what he had said, "Date TBA." Everyone laughed even louder this time.

Ian placed the two-carat diamond ring on the middle finger of her left hand. Then he stood up without help, stepped to the bed, and kissed her.

The doctor and Mrs. Lawrence politely excused themselves from Ian and their daughter and drove home.

"How did you know the exact size of the ring I wear?"

"That's top secret," Ian said as he handed her the blue box the ring came in.

"I know the top secret. She just left here with my Dad."

"Don't blame your mother, Kaitlin. I've known her for about a year, and she's a good person."

"How did you meet my mother?"

"She had been shopping at Walls-Mart, and one day, as she came out of the store, someone was trying to break into her car. I could see she was distressed. I stopped and arrested the hoodlum for attempted breaking and entering, and she drove home safely."

"And my dad?"

"He stopped me when I was coming down Purcell Road one time and identified himself. Then he informed me he needed transportation to the ER, and I took him. That was about a year ago."

"And all this time, they never said a word about knowing you. I think there's a name for this engagement."

"It's called a conspiracy to commit marriage. Date TBA." They laughed.

"This should be good for a cartoon or two. Imagine two blocks. In the first block, there's a man on bended knee asking his girl to marry him. In the second block, the girl says she will marry him, but at a date TBA (to be announced)."

"Is everything we do going to be in cartoon form?" He asked with a smile on his face.

"No way, Ian. What we do will not be put into cartoon form. At least, I hope it won't. What's that sound?"

"That sound alerts everyone that it's time for the visitors to depart."

"Guess I had better leave." Kaitlin turned toward the door after giving Ian a kiss.

"Kaitlin. Don't worry. We'll have a good life together, and it won't be dull."

"See you later, TBA," Kaitlin said and then left the room.

He smiled, then looked through his mail. Most of it was advertisements, but two pieces interested him. One was the newspaper article on President Biden denying chocolate milk to US schoolchildren, and the other was on his G7 trip to Japan, where the main subject was a woman's right to have an abortion and those against it were a threat to democracy.

"What was it he called Republicans who believed in making America great again? Despicable and deserving of hate and contempt. Let's see what he has accomplished. He put us into a recession, weaponized the FBI in order to stop President T from running for President, and opened our borders so fentanyl could kill our young people. Then he runs for reelection. And that's only part of what he has accomplished." Then came a knock on the door.

"Are you awake, Mister Drenn?" It was the nurse dispensing the evening medication.

"Open your mouth, please." He did, and she dropped a pill in it, then handed him a glass of water to drink to ensure he swallowed the pill.

Chapter Ten

Eight long days later, Kaitlin returned home after completing her assignment, and she didn't call or see Ian. Sitting in the kitchen on a Tuesday morning, she was in deep thought when her mother entered the room. "Morning, Mom."

"Good morning, Dear. Do you feel alright?"

"Why do you ask, Mom?" Tears were streaming down her cheeks.

"I can tell something is bothering you. Did something happen while on this last assignment you need to talk about?"

Her head bowed, she struggled for the words to explain her behavior. "Mom, do you remember Sean Morris?" She wiped the tears from her eyes.

"Yes. I think so. He was a schoolteacher."

"We were married three days ago, and he'll be here Friday to pick me up." She appeared troubled. "Mom, on our wedding night, he wore a blond wig and a gown nicer than mine. There was no sex; he's a man's man, and what am I going to do about Ian?"

"You should have thought about him a week ago, Kaitlin. I believe you should return his ring. That should be explanation enough."

"I'll give the ring back to Ian. Sean Morris married me just to give him legitimacy with the School Board!"

"I was talking about Sean's ring, and you should get packed, Dear. Friday is just around the corner."

"Mom, did I hurt you, and will Dad accept Sean?"

"That's to be seen, Dear." Mrs. Lawrence poured herself a cup of hot tea.

Ian had driven by the Lawrence house many times and knew exactly when Kaitlin returned home. He did not telephone her, and she didn't contact him. He finally realized that she no longer wanted him. He was alone and hurting. Today was Friday, and he let the telephone ring and ring until he finally answered it.

When a beautiful woman cries, you can hear it echo through the halls of time, but when a man cries, it covers the sorrow of being alone.

"Ian, this is Kaitlin; we need to talk."

"Alright. Where?"

"My house."

"I'm walking out of the door now." A cool breeze was blowing in from the southwest, and he felt a cold chill across the back of his neck.

Mrs. Lawrence heard the knock on her front door and opened it to see Ian. She didn't have a smile on her face, and he quickly realized something was wrong.

Kaitlin addressed him in a business tone of voice. "Ian, this is Sean. My husband."

Ian's beliefs were confirmed, and he turned on the charm. He smiled, as if happy for her. "Well," he said, "congratulations." He held out his hand to Sean, and they shook hands. Ian immediately felt Sean Morris's handshake was as limp as a wet wash rag, and he smelled of perfume. "*Well, maybe I was wrong about Kaitlin,*" he thought.

He then turned to Kaitlin and said, "I wish you the best, Kaitlin. I know you will be happy," and they hugged. It was then that she passed the ring to him without Sean seeing it.

"Mrs. Lawrence, do you have any hot tea in the kitchen? It's a little nippy out there."

"Yes, I do. Follow me." Ian trailed her to the kitchen and watched as she poured him a cup of tea and put a slice of lemon on the saucer.

"Have a seat, Ian." He squeezed the slice of lemon into the steaming hot cup of tea and stirred it.

Mrs. Lawrence sat across from him, stirring her cup of tea. "I don't know what got into her, Ian. The guy's a three-dollar bill."

"I remember what my father used to tell me when playing the game of football. *You win some, you lose some, and some get rained out.* I can only assume he was in the right place at the right time. At least he smells good, Mrs. Lawrence." He smiled.

"You're taking this better than I thought, Ian. You're hurting. I can tell."

"Mrs. Lawrence, I'm crying on the inside,"—he stood up– "but I've got places to go and people to see. Thank you for the tea. I know the way out."

He placed his cup and saucer in the sink, then walked out of the kitchen and out the front door with a smile on his face that turned to a laugh.

He turned the evergreen-colored Cadillac toward US 401 and turned north. Within minutes, he was on US 74, traveling west to Rockingham and the Cadillac dealers.

"Why do you want to trade, Mister Drenn?" The salesman asked. "This is practically a new car."

"I need one a bit larger," Ian said. "I like that one over there," he added, pointing to another evergreen-colored Cadillac.

"Well, if you come inside, we'll do the paperwork. How do you want to pay for it, Mister Drenn?"

"Can we do an electronic transfer?" Ian asked.

"Yes, sir." It didn't take long for the paperwork to be finished and another half hour for the car to be inspected. They filled up the gas tank and parked it in front of the office for him to see.

"Mister Drenn, we're finished," the salesman said, handing Ian the keys and a stack of papers. "All that you had in the vehicle was transferred to your trunk."

"Thank you, Mister Spicer. If I want another car, I'll come to you. You do good work." He praised the car salesman and drove out of the lot.

For a few moments, he felt the hurt Kaitlin had put him through. But he was able to settle down and accept what had happened.

At home, he threw a protective cover over the car, then fixed himself a sandwich and opened a small bottle of Coke. He finally found a comfortable spot on the sofa and turned on the television. After eating, he slept for an hour.

At about four o'clock, he telephoned Richard En, a communications technician used by law enforcement agencies in five counties.

"Rick, this is Ian Drenn. I need some cameras installed in my new car. Can you help me?"

"Drenn, I'm up to my ears in work now. Can I help you next Thursday?"

"You read my mind. Bring it in at about 8 a.m.?"

"That's right, but if I get an opening, I'll call you. Are you still at 277-1786?"

"Correct," Ian replied.

"See you then. Out."

The phone went silent except for the dial tone, and Ian hung up the telephone.

Early Thursday morning, Ian dressed in gym clothes and drove the Cadillac to Rick En's business shop.

"It's going to take most of the day, Drenn. Are you going to wait?"

"No. I'm going to try and walk home if you can get someone to bring me the car, and I will pay them and return them to here?"

"I can do that. You want the good stuff?"

"Yep," he echoed Kaitlin.

"You know it's five miles back to your place?"

"Is that all?" Drenn asked. "Then I'd better get started." He had a smile on his face and waved at Rick En as he turned away from him.

"See you at about five thirty, Drenn."

"I'll be awake," he answered, turning around to start his long walk home. When he arrived at where Purcell Road meets Blues Farm Road, he started to jog. His stride was perfect, his breathing was steady, the pain existed but he dealt with it, and the world opened up to him as he increased his speed. When he could see his house from a distance, he slowed down to a steady walk. Before he knew it, he was home and feeling good.

After a warm shower, he dressed in casual clothing, then raided the refrigerator, pouring himself a small glass of white milk and eating two Oreo cookies.

His car arrived at five fifty, and he handed Rick En a handful of hundred-dollar bills. En counted them and said, "That will take care of it. Now let me show you how it works." Drenn watched and listened as Rick En educated him.

"Push button A to turn it on, and you will get a picture up front. Button B and you get front and back; Button C turns it off. If you want to pinpoint a particular thing in your field of view, hold the button down. When you want to return the view to its normal position, just take your finger off the button. To photograph something in your field of view, press Button D. Your photograph will be a still shot, and it will come out on the left side. If you are photographing on Channel B, you will get two pictures. Now there is a way to adjust the cameras, but you should have someone who knows how to do the work do it. Understand?"

"Got it," Drenn said and came down from the car, closing the door. He protected the car's finish by throwing a cover over it.

At 7 p.m., he turned on the nightly news and watched as the Secretary of the Department of Homeland Security took credit for slowing down the number of illegal migrants coming into the United States. He failed to mention the seven hundred thousand that escaped the Customs Border Patrol and are hiding somewhere in the United States, possibly waiting for directions from Russia or China. *"I think Congress should impeach him,"* Ian thought.

The early Saturday morning frost covered most of the lawns in the area. Ian was ready for breakfast at Biscuitvalley.

However, at the Lawrence residence, Kaitlin had decided not to leave with her new husband but to seek an annulment of the marriage on Monday morning. She and her mother sat at the kitchen table and discussed what she should do.

"Mom, is it possible to win Ian back?"

"I don't know if that's possible, dear. Perhaps – and I say just perhaps – if I can talk to him, I can convince him you were out of your mind or just plain crazy! But I have this idea that Ian Scott Drenn already knows what happened to you. And he's probably still laughing."

"I know I hurt him, but what can I do to regain his trust?" Her hands were folding a dishcloth. "And I don't even remember getting married."

"Ian has a great deal of pride, Dear. You hurt his pride because he believed in you enough to ask you to be his wife. I can think of two ways it may be possible for you to regain his trust. But first, I must know how bad you want him back."

"Mom, I'll do all that I can to get him back. It's Ian I love."

"Are you ready to go back to work?"

"I'm going to try and work, Mom. I don't know if I can be objective anymore. This thing with Sean Morris and Ian has hit me hard. I just don't feel good about myself."

"You've lost confidence in your ability to do your job?"

"I think that if I knew Ian would take me back, I could go back to work."

"It's too early to even think about that, dear. You've torn down the trust he had in you. Do you think he's going to say that's alright? I love you. Ian's not that way, dear."

"Let me ask you this. Are you a cartoonist or not?"

"I am, Mom."

"Then why not use your abilities to draw an apology to Ian and a promise to do better? That would be a starting point."

"Silent communications," Kaitlin muttered to herself.

"Draw a block of twelve cartoons, and I will pay to have it placed in the paper. We should run it for about five days. That would be a start."

"What if that doesn't work, Mom?"

"Then we'll try something else," her mother answered.

A week later, Kaitlin submitted her artwork to the Scotland Exchange newspaper, and three days after that, it was published.

Ian heard his telephone ring and just picked it up before Richard En hung up.

"Hello," Ian said, almost out of breath.

"Ian, this is Richard En. Look, buddy, we've known each other for about three years now, and you've got to do something."

"What on earth are you talking about?"

"Don't you read the papers?" Richard asked and waited for Ian to answer.

"I haven't read the paper in the last two or three days. Why?"

"Do you have today's newspaper?"

"Yes." He thumbed through some letters before getting to the newspaper.

"Well, read it! Page three!"

Ian Scott Drenn picked up the newspaper and turned to page three. Then he started laughing. "Okay, Richard. I understand and will contact her."

"You know her?"

"Yes. I asked her to marry me a long time ago."

"Alright. See you later, Drenn." He hung up the telephone. As soon as Ian hung up, the phone rang again.

"Drenn speaking."

"Drenn? This is Chief. Have you read today's newspaper?"

"Yes, Sir."

"Do you know the girl who drew this cartoon, and is she talking about you and her?"

"I know the girl very well, Chief."

"Well, it's none of my business, but I advise you to contact her. Immediately."

"I'll take care of it, Chief Darby, and thanks for calling."

By the end of the day, Ian Scott Drenn had received twenty-seven telephone calls, all encouraging him to contact Kaitlin. His answer was the same to all who called: "Thank you for calling; I will contact her very soon."

Before going to bed that night, he disconnected the telephone so he could get some sleep.

Then on Friday, he received the one hundredth phone call. It was from Aunt Dee's Bakery. "Mister Drenn. Give this girl a call. She deserves another chance. There are ten people in the bakery who all say the same thing. And if you call her, I'll give you a fresh apple pie with cinnamon on it. Bye, Mister Drenn." He laughed but wanted more than just an apology. He desired to know how it came to be in the first place, and her cartoons didn't explain that.

That weekend, he took the Cadillac to get it thoroughly cleaned in Fayetteville, then drove to Raleigh only to discover the Capital Newspaper had picked up Kaitlin's cartoon. Not only had Raleigh picked up the cartoons, but Durham, Greensboro, and Charlotte.

Driving home on US 74 on Sunday morning, he decided he had better call Mrs. Lawrence and inquire as to how Kaitlin came to marry Sean Morris.

At two o'clock, he telephoned Mrs. Lawrence, and she suggested they meet. In the Lawrence home kitchen, he drank a cup of hot tea with a twist of lemon in it and listened to Mrs. Lawrence explain the situation to him and her husband. Both laughed.

Kaitlin's boss had reassigned her to another candidate, and she was covering a rally in the mountains of western Virginia. "She will not return until tomorrow," Mrs. Lawrence told Ian, "and the second section of cartoons will be published Monday. It will cover just what I've told you."

"And I'll get another hundred telephone calls," Ian said to Mrs. Lawrence. "You know her cartoons have been picked up in Raleigh, Durham, Greensboro, and Charlotte. I just hope I don't start getting telephone calls from them." He took a deep breath. "I'll call Kaitlin once she comes in. Maybe take her for a ride in the T-Bird. See you later, and thanks."

He drove north on US 401 and stopped at the car wash to give the Cadillac a well-deserved seven-dollar clean-up.

The next afternoon, he telephoned Kaitlin, and they agreed to meet. He drove the new car to her house and waited for her to come outside.

Kaitlin and her mother had been waiting for him to park in their driveway. He was halfway to the porch when Kaitlin came out and walked to him. He had a smile on his face, and she understood that all was forgiven.

"Your mother told me how it happened. Some people are jealous of your accomplishments. Did your mother tell you the newspapers picked up your cartoons about us in Raleigh, Durham, Greensboro, and Charlotte?" he asked.

"I just found out about it. So, the whole State knew about our situation." They laughed as they embraced, and then kissed before walking to the car.

"Where are we going?" she asked.

He drove to Aunt Dee's Bakery. "Aunt Dee, I'm Ian Drenn, and this is Kaitlin Lawrence, the cartoonist. I've come for an apple pie with cinnamon on it."

You would have believed it was New Year's Eve, and the clock had just struck midnight when Aunt Dee announced who they were. Customers joyfully applauded and gave off cheerful shouts of good luck and happy times. Pictures were taken by Aunt Dee's customers, and Aunt Dee presented Ian and Kaitlin with a hot pie right out of the oven, sprinkled with cinnamon, and then placed it in a cardboard box.

"Thank you for coming, Mister Drenn. Is she the artist?" Aunt Dee asked.

"Yes," and he leaned over to whisper in her ear. "And we will get married. I just don't know when Aunt Dee."

"Thank you, and I wish the two of you all the luck in the world."

"Thank you." Kaitlin and Ian echoed as they departed the bakery, waving at the customers.

Inside the car, Kaitlin asked, "Someday, you will have to tell me what that trip was all about. It was not about getting a pie, was it?"

"No. It concerned a telephone call based on your cartoons."

"You're kidding?"

"I'm not kidding. Do you understand that your cartoons brought unity among the people who read the newspapers in a half dozen communities?" he asked, then continued to say, "Over the week your first block of cartoons were depicted, I received approximately three hundred telephone calls telling me to contact you. I've never seen anything like that."

He started the car and drove south on Main Street, passing his bank and the doughnut place, before Kaitlin inquired, "Do you know of Senator Scott of Carolina? The one running for president?" Kaitlin asked.

"Yes. He's the guy talking about unity. I've heard him, and he's got a great message for the people."

Drenn turned right onto West Boulevard. "Do you think he will be elected?" Kaitlin wanted his opinion.

"He's three strikes against him. First, hate and the preachers of hate and racism are very politically powerful. Second, the feeling of hope has been replaced by a feeling of skepticism because of the mistrust of the Biden Administration, and lastly, the uncertainty of having a paycheck tomorrow. He needs money to get his all-important message spread across this nation. But if he is elected, it's a start in making America great again."

"Now you sound like that other person running for President. What's his name?"

"You know, Kaitlin, with your ability to bring people together with art, you could help Scott get his message across. We need what he's selling."

"I don't know if my employer would like that, Ian. He tells me the slant I must use to create my cartoons. Or I don't get paid." Kaitlin informed him.

"Let me ask you this. Could you create a pamphlet depicting Scott's message without your boss knowing it?"

"I could, but my artwork is also a fingerprint. He would make a direct connection between what I am being paid to do and what I do on my own. It would be a conflict of interest. And that's not good if I want to continue to work."

"I see," Drenn said. Then he asked, "Do you need anything before I take you home?"

"You could feed me. There's a place on the left just ahead." Kaitlin smiled and saw Ian nod his head, indicating it was time to eat.

Just before turning onto the US 401 by-pass, Drenn turned left and drove into the restaurant's parking area.

It was a cafeteria-style business, and they quickly decided what they wanted to eat and found an open table.

"Have you heard anything about your annulment, Kaitlin?" Ian asked while cutting a piece of well-done meat.

"I should know something by Thursday. My lawyer telephoned my mother and gave her an appointment time. Would you like to be there?" Kaitlin asked because she wanted him to hear what the lawyer had to say.

"I most certainly would. Do me a favor, will you?"

"What can I do for you?" Kaitlin wanted to know.

"Draw a cartoon explaining what the lawyer tells you. The people of this area deserve an explanation and closure. I would estimate that thousands of people have read the cartoons you ran in the paper."

"Do you really think they would read it?" She questioned his reasoning.

"I know they would enjoy reading it because of the response to the first artwork."

"Let's see what the lawyer has to say first. It may be something bad," she countered. "But if it's a good report, I'll do it. You pay for it."

"Agreed," he said with a smile on his face.

They finished eating and were on their way to Kaitlin's house when he told her something that may have helped.

"Kaitlin. Sometimes, jealous competitors do their best to hurt others who are better than they are. Whatever happens on Thursday afternoon, keep your chin up. You are exceptionally good at your job, and that may have been the reason others tried to do you harm. Don't let them destroy your confidence. Understand?"

"I do understand, Ian, and thank you for saying that." Kaitlin said, "Home is where the heart is."

"We are where your heart is." Ian laughed and stopped the car in the driveway, then opened the door for her to exit.

"You're a gentleman, Ian," she said and gently kissed him.

Ian smiled, thinking of Kaitlin as he drove further down Purcell Road. *Home, at last*, he thought as he pulled into the carport.

For the past three weeks, Ian had been constructing a project in his backyard. It was a game of horseshoes, and he didn't know anyone in the area who played such an old game. He figured there must be an old farmer in the area who played the game at one time or another. That was the reason he hand-built two backboards and cemented two steel stakes into the ground at the required distance. But he could not remember the scoring process. "*Perhaps I should check the internet for instructions*," he thought as he changed into some old work clothes.

He had found four commercial horseshoes at a yard sale and repainted two of them red and the other two blue as required. He tested them with one finger to see if they were dry and found they were.

For the rest of the cloudy afternoon, he practiced throwing horseshoes from one stake to the other. Getting one ringer out of twelve tosses clearly indicated he needed lots of practice.

As he leisurely walked back into the house, he was aware of the change in weather. The clouds were getting darker, and he felt it might rain. After washing his hands and changing clothes, he found a comfortable spot on the sofa, turned on the television, and then turned it off. He was feeling uneasy. He walked to the sunroom, where his laptop computer was, and began to type.

Open Letter #1

Dear Sons and Daughters,

Once upon a time, a Socialist-Democrat tiger prowled the streets of Laurinburg, looking for easy prey. He came to a man, looked him up and down, then loudly growled, terrifying even himself.

At once, the man dropped to his knees and begged the tiger not to harm him. With one powerful swipe of the tiger's paw, the man's life ended. The tiger felt good about himself and continued to prowl among people who had assembled to learn, pray, and expose their weaknesses. He terminated all of them.

Then, he came to a man and his family who wanted to negotiate. He smiled. This was something new. "I'll give you my wife, my child, my land, and even my dog if you will stop killing," the man offered. "I'll do all I can for you. I know we can come to some arrangement." The poor old dog looked up at the man with eyes of dismay, then slumped back to the floor.

The tiger laughed as tigers do and deprived them all of life, liberty, and happiness. The tiger slowly walked to Purcell Road and growled at an old man who lived there.

The old man immediately grabbed the tiger by its throat while removing a ball-point pen from his shirt pocket, then proceeded to beat the tiger from the top of its head to the tip of its tail, inside out and outside in, from left to right, then pulled the claws from the tiger's paws one at a time.

While the tiger lay trembling on Purcell Road, the old man went to the tiger's den. There he trashed its computer, shredded its hammer and sickle-adorned flag, and threw its television set into Gum Swamp. To add insult to injury, the old man made a parking lot on top of its den and then returned.

With his right hand, the old man gripped the tiger by its throat and, with his other hand, pinned a note to its chest.

The note stated:

"This is my land. From sea to glimmering sea. If you mess with it, you mess with me!"

The shivering Socialist-Democrat tiger thought for a second. "You must be one of those despicable Republicans or flag-waving Democrats we were warned about." He never prowled the streets of Laurinburg again.

The moral of this story is:

When dealing with people living on Purcell Road, tigers, bad guys, and Socialist-Democrats, you first must win the argument, then you can win the vote!

When true Democrats vote on the straight Democratic ticket, the Socialists win, not America.

Love,

Dad

Ian laughed at what he had just written, then closed down the laptop computer and went to bed. His thoughts were of beautiful Kaitlin, and he wondered just how much longer he had to be alone.

Chapter Eleven

The Made-in-Laurinburg-North Carolina clock's alarm announced the start of another day. He turned off the alarm and rolled out of a warm bed, only to see three frisky squirrels playing in the backyard when he looked out of the bathroom window.

At 7 a.m., he met Kaitlin at the mailbox, and they walked for a mile, then jogged back. "Would you like to come in? Maybe rest a bit," he offered.

"Yes, I need to rest and see what the inside of your house looks like." They walked in. "The last time I was in here, I had to use the bathroom and didn't get a chance to see everything." Ian held the door open for her.

"Orange juice?" he asked.

"Yes," she responded, and Ian poured two small glasses of cold orange juice and handed one to her. "Go ahead and wander through the house."

She sipped on the glass of juice as she looked into each room. When she had finished, she joined Ian on the sofa that needed to be replaced.

"So, what have you been doing?" She placed her glass on a paper napkin that was on the coffee table and tried to relax on the old sofa.

"Hmmm, for the last couple of weeks, I have been building a place where I can play horseshoes."

"Horseshoes? Do you have a horse hidden somewhere?"

He laughed. "Look out back," he said. "Do you see the two wooden backboards with the steel stakes in the ground?"

"Yes."

"Well, when you play the game of horseshoes, you are trying to throw one or two horseshoes around that steel stake. If you do get a ringer, that counts for some points. Got it?"

"Yes. Have you tried to get a ringer yet?"

"Of course. I got one ringer out of twelve tosses."

She laughed. "It sounds like you need a lot of practice, Ian."

"Well, maybe. Would you like to try it?"

"Not now. I'm tired. Can I just rest for a while?"

"Of course. If you need me, I'll be at the other end of the sofa." It was the first time they slept together. Drenn slept at one end of the old sofa, and Kaitlin at the other end.

When he awoke, Kaitlin was gone, and it was nearly noon. "I slept for almost three hours," he said to himself. "I must have been tired."

An hour later, the house telephone rang, and Ian answered it. "Drenn's residence."

"Drenn? Ian Scott Drenn? This is Tom Spevere."

"Well, I'll be a monkey's uncle. How long has it been?"

"Three long years, Ian."

"Where are you, and what are you doing?"

"I'm in Hawaii, and I'm an electrician working for the Air Force. I heard you were a police officer?"

"Medically retired police officer. It's open season on cops nowadays!"

"Is it bad?"

"No."

"Look, buddy, we're going to have to get together. I'm coming back to Arizona. On May 23, you can help us celebrate our third wedding anniversary.

"I'll be there, Tom."

"Take care, Ian. See you then. Bye."

"Bye, Tom." He hung up the phone and remembered their last year at Richmond Tech. *"It was nice hearing from him,"* he thought.

He dialed Kaitlin's number, and when she answered, he said, "Hi, what are you doing?"

"Just got off the telephone, Ian. What time did you awaken?"

"About eleven or around that time," he replied. "What time did you leave?"

"About ten. We must have been tired," she said. "I miss you."

"I know, but we'll be together soon. I've got the feeling everything is not as it seems, but we'll see tomorrow."

"What makes you say that?"

"I don't have any inside information, but I understand in your business, you have a lot of competition. Sometimes people are extremely jealous and create false situations to bring down the reputation of good people like yourself."

"We'll know tomorrow, Ian, whether I am a good person or not."

"I don't believe that for one minute, Kaitlin. You are a good person. Don't let anybody tell you differently. You're probably being framed."

"You think so?" she sounded concerned.

"Yes. I was a policeman once, remember?"

"Thank you, Ian. I'll see you tomorrow at noon plus thirty."

"Are you buying lunch?" he smiled to himself.

"After seeing the lawyer, I'll take you and Mom to a late lunch of hamburgers and a Coke," she said jokingly.

He laughed. "I can hardly wait." He paused, waiting for her to say something.

"Good night, Ian."

"Good night, Honey."

Ian carefully pulled his car into the Lawrence driveway at exactly twelve thirty p.m. He wore a lightweight black suit with a light blue turtleneck sweater. He saw a smile on Kaitlin's face as she and her mother walked out onto the street. He held the door open for her mother to sit next to the driver while Kaitlin sat in the back seat.

It took them fifteen minutes or less to drive to the lawyer's office and another fifteen minutes to get comfortable in his less busy office. Then, his secretary motioned for them to enter her boss's domain.

Introductions were made, and the lawyer remembered Ian Drenn from previous criminal cases he had handled.

"The question is, are you legally married to Sean Morris? He looked at Kaitlin and continued. And the answer is no. You were never married to Sean Morris. I visited your hotel, and you don't owe them any money. I visited the novelty shop across the street and obtained an exact copy of your so-called marriage license for four dollars and sixty-three cents. I also checked with the hotel's security section and arranged to have a copy of the footage taken of the people you were with. Further investigation clearly shows they are your fellow cartoonists. It depicts that your drink had something added to it. What? We'll never know. My question to you is, what do you want done?"

"Is it possible to obtain a picture of the person who drugged me?" Kaitlin wanted to know.

The lawyer remained silent and instead handed her a ten-by-twelve-inch photograph. He waited as she studied the picture. Then he asked, "Do you know this individual?"

"Yes. His name is Oxford Haystacker, and he works for a competitor in Chicago."

That's when Ian spoke up. "Excuse me, Kaitlin." He turned to the lawyer. "What are the chances of proving a felony in this case?"

"From what I've seen here and the evidence I've collected, the chances are far greater to bring a case like this to court. I wouldn't even try just based on the lack of evidence and statute of limitations." He observed that Kaitlin was thinking about something, but he didn't know what it was. He turned to Ian. "I cannot tell you what to do, but I think you know how to handle this situation?"

"I do," Ian replied. "And hope I get the chance."

"What are you doing for a living, Mr. Drenn?" the lawyer asked.

"I received my P.I. license the day before yesterday," he replied.

"Are we finished, Ms. Lawrence? By the way, I like your cartoons."

"We are finished and thank you. Do I owe you any money?"

"No. Your generous retainer covered everything." He stood from behind his desk and held the door open for them to leave.

In Ian's new Cadillac, it was decided they would eat a late lunch at the restaurant across the street from the busy Walls-Mart.

Afterward, he drove to the Lawrences' home, where he was invited to come in. Sitting at the kitchen table, Kaitlin asked, "Ian, what did the lawyer mean when he said you would know how to handle this?"

"There's a way for Mister Hay stacker to pay for his misdeeds; however, you should not be involved."

"Why?"

"Because if something happens, you would be a suspect."

"Oooh," she said. "What would happen to repay him for his dirty deeds?"

"Does he drive a car to these rallies?"

"Yes. A blue and gray BMW convertible."

"Then this is a weakness that could be targeted."

"You target weaknesses?"

"Correct." He paused. "The easy weakness in a car is its tires and fuel. This being a convertible adds another weakness to the list. The weakness in a hotel room may be a bed full of cockroaches or a non-harmful snake. Understand?"

"Yes, I got it," she smiled.

"You've got work to do, Kaitlin. Thousands of people are waiting for your cartoon depicting the outcome of your meeting with your lawyer. You're an exceptional artist, Kaitlin. Are you sure about us?"

"Yes, I'm sure."

With Kaitlin's mother watching Ian, he said, "By the power of the kitchen table, I again ask you to marry me. The date and time TBA."

Kaitlin smiled and answered. "By the power of the kitchen table, I again accept. Date and time TBA."

All three of them laughed as Ian placed the diamond ring on Kaitlin's middle left finger, and then they kissed.

Chapter Twelve

That night, the rain danced across the roof, creating a pattern of calming music, and Ian slept like a baby. Friday morning, he stayed in bed until ten o'clock and arose only when he heard someone knocking on the front door. It was Kaitlin, and he was still in his pajamas when he answered the door. He unlocked the glass storm door and held it open for her to enter.

She took one look at his pajamas and asked, "Where on earth did you get those pajamas?"

"And what's wrong with my pajamas?"

"Well, I don't know if they are red with white dots or white with red dots. Where did you get them?"

"I'll have you know I ordered these out of the Ward's Catalog and paid a whole forty dollars for them."

She laughed. "Were they on sale?"

"Yes, and I like them."

"At least now I know what to buy you for Christmas."

"I thought you would take me out for breakfast, but I see you're not presentable."

"What do you mean, not presentable? Get in the car. We're going to Biscuitvalley." He dared her to go with him.

"We go," and she walked with him to the car. He was in his pajamas, and she was laughing all the way there. He bought two breakfast platters with bacon and grits, no butter. He ordered orange juice to wash it all down and paid for it with cash.

"You know this is going to put weight on you, don't you?"

"I'll work it off."

"Okay, if I ask you a personal question, Ian?"

"Kaitlin, you may ask me questions, but if I don't answer them, it's because there's a very good reason not to. Understood?"

"Yes, do you have a gun?"

"Of course, I do, and I know how and when to use it."

They returned to Ian's house.

"When you faced the twelve-year-old boy pointing a gun at you, did you think about killing him?"

They were sitting at the dining room table at this time.

"No, I tried to talk him into making a mistake. I never considered killing a young boy who was being misled by the adults in the room."

"You were willing to be killed rather than kill a child?"

"Today, every person that wears the uniform of a law enforcement officer is a target for some punk wielding a firearm, knife, or some other weapon. There are people out there that will do anything to degrade an officer of the law."

"You wore the uniform. Why?"

"I became a police officer to help those who couldn't help themselves, to stop crime, and during the summer to assist those in the Police Athletic League."

"Now is it alright if I ask you a question?"

"If it's not too personal, you can ask, Ian."

"When am I going to see you in your pajamas?"

She laughed, then became serious. "Give me six months, Ian. The election will be decided long before November. Biden will stay in the Rose Gar- den and run his campaign from there. His opponent will be with the people trying to get his message across because the mainstream media won't treat him equally as Biden or whoever else the Russians or Chinese have bought."

"Six months is a long time, but I'm willing to wait to see you in your PJs." This made her laugh.

"You can bet they are not spotted like yours," she said while Ian held open a white plastic trash bag as Kaitlin cleaned off the table.

"You really believe the Chinese and Russians control Biden?"

"That's my opinion, Ian. Whether it's true or not is something else. But that's the way it looks."

"Then we agree on that. I listened to the television news last night before going to bed and heard that Bank of Amerika has been giving the lists of names of people who paid for guns with a check or made an electronic transfer to the Federal Bureau of Investigation. The gun owners of America and the people of the United States are under attack by whoever is pulling Biden's rope." Ian was sitting on the sofa.

"If you put it that way, the fact that China killed a million of our citizens with COVID-19 and they're behind the fentanyl being smuggled into the US to kill and cause harm to our families, it all adds up," Kaitlin added, and sat on the sofa next to him.

"We're always talking politics, Kaitlin. How about us? You and me. The future." He wrapped his arm around her shoulders, and she cuddled closer to him. "I like what I'm doing, Ian, but I'm willing to trade it for a wedding ring in due time." She kissed him, and he returned her kiss. "It's nice being with you, Ian, but I've finished my work for its next publication, and I thought we could just spend some time together."

"Should I get dressed or undressed for you?" He smiled.

"By all means, get dressed, and if you can feed me, then we can do something."

"I've got just the thing," he said and disappeared into his bedroom, only to reappear fully dressed, wearing a leather jacket, and carrying another jacket in his hands. "Let's go, Honey."

"Yes, Dear." She followed him to the secure building housing the 1956 Ford T-Bird. Within minutes, they were headed to eat lunch at the restaurant across the street from a continuously busy Walls-Mart parking lot.

"Where are we going?" Kaitlin asked while wrapping a scarf around her head to keep her hair from being messed up.

"To do some fishing without hooks," he said while driving through Whiteville.

"How do you expect to catch fish without hooks?"

"We're not fishing for fish," he responded.

"We're not going to fish, but for something other than fish, so we're fishing for sunken treasure?" Kaitlin surmised.

"Yep," he mocked her.

They arrived in Calabash, and he drove to the wooden pier. Ian removed a small Army pack from the trunk of his car, then opened the door for Kaitlin, leading the way onto the pier.

From the pack, he removed two large magnets with ropes attached to them. "Okay, this is what we do. Unroll the rope and tie one end to your left wrist. Then, with your right hand, lower or toss the magnet into the water. What you retrieve, you may keep as a treasure."

She laughed. "You're crazy," she said, doing as he instructed. Soon, she yelled to Ian, "Hey, look what I got!" She had pulled up a rod and reel from the sea floor.

Ian inspected her find and said, "By the power of the kitchen table, I officially dub you a treasure hunter!" She laughed, and as they worked their way along the pier, item after item was pulled from the salt water.

"What are we going to do with all of this stuff, Ian?" she asked, astonished by all that they had retrieved.

"I do not need for any of it. Do you?"

"I would like to keep a souvenir, Ian," Kaitlin told him.

"May I suggest the reel from the rod? It would remind us of our first treasure-hunting expedition."

"Good idea. What's a reel?"

"Here," and he picked up a rod with a reel attached to it and, within seconds, removed the reel and handed it to her.

"Would you like to eat seafood before driving home?" Ian asked while putting everything back into his car.

"No, I don't think so, but the next time we're here, we will," she said while getting into the T-Bird. "It's going to be dark soon, Ian."

Ian put the pedal to the metal and, fortunately, wasn't caught by the NC Highway Patrol. When they arrived in Laurinburg, Kaitlin was still holding the reel. He pulled up in front of the Lawrences' home.

"Ian, I want to do this again. I've never been treasure-hunting before, and I had a lot of fun."

"Honey, there's a lot of places to investigate for lost treasures. I enjoyed being with you."

Before Kaitlin got out of the little car, they kissed. "If you're serious about treasure hunting, I'll call for you at eight o'clock tomorrow."

"Let's do it," she said before disappearing into her parents' home.

"*You know there must be something wrong with me. Every time I'm with Kaitlin, we talk politics, and it takes my mind from her,*" he thought to himself while driving home.

He parked the T-Bird and tossed a protective cover over it.

Inside the house, he washed his hands, fixed himself a grilled cheese sandwich, and opened a small bottle of Coke. Then he made his way to the sunroom and sat behind his laptop computer. "*I wonder if I can type another open letter?*" he thought and started to type, using two fingers to do the talking.

Open Letter #2

I am your Socialist-Democrat Tiger President. You elected me and others like me to care for you, your family, and your friends from the time you were born until you die.

Because the North Carolina state government appears racist to me and out of control today, I am revoking Amendment X and assuming the powers of the state government.

In order to have an orderly transfer of power, I have appointed the United Nations Civil Affairs Division to be in charge of your State. Give them your cooperation, your young children to be reeducated, and your firearms to stop crime.

To further reorganize government in the lower forty-nine states (Washington, DC, is granted statehood), they are separated into regions. As you can see, North Carolina is in Region Six.

Region Six: Mississippi, Alabama, Georgia, Florida, South Carolina, and North Carolina.

I further decree that Hawaii, Midway, and Guam be returned to China, and Alaska to Russia. No one will leave their assigned State without written permission from State and Region Commanders.

The flag known as Old Glory will no longer be displayed. Only the new United Socialist States of America (USSA) flag will be flown.

It was brought to my attention that, in order to form a more perfect union, the Constitution of the United States needs to be rewritten because the current one is far outdated. To rectify this, I have decreed that Congress write a new Constitution pending my approval.

I have purposely closed all places of worship because of unhealthy verbal exchanges and the inability to come together as one. It was brought to my attention that Christians desire to pray on Sunday, and anti-Christians do not pray on that day. I have directed military Chaplains to perform same-sex marriages in Christian chapels or face court-martial charges. Homosexuality is no longer a sin, and the Bible will no longer be quoted. I decree that religious liberty be null and void.

I've increased the harassment of former President T and his MAGA supporters. The red baseball cap with MAGA on it is now outlawed. I have called President T's supporters stupid, half-witted, dumb, brainless, and despicable, all for you, and that includes former military and naval retired personnel.

Because of the food shortage, I have decreed that food will be supplied only on Wednesdays, in order of age. The youngest first. The old do not need food because they will soon die.

Farmers who have declared they will not follow my orders will be sent to reeducation camps. No individual will eat more than what is provided to him/her/other. Anyone caught with seeds will be prosecuted.

Armed personnel will control food production because everyone who elected me wanted to be equal to their next-door neighbor.

Thank you for your peaceful cooperation. Have a nice day.
Signed:
Your loving President, Joe.

I've completely worn out my two fingers writing this, he thought. "I just wonder if the people of the United States know their decision to elect Biden President has brought us closer to a world war. All because of his pride. His pride in his weak son is a weakness that was exploited by not only Russia's Intelligence but China's too."

He picked up the house phone and called Kaitlin. When she answered, he said, "Kaitlin, would you like to hunt for rubies, emeralds, and sapphires? And maybe gold?"

"Are you out of your mind?" she asked, thinking he had been drinking.

"I'm talking about a drive to the mountains. Somewhere around Cherokee and Franklin. An overnight stay, so bring your PJs and a change of clothing because you're going to get dirty."

"No hanky-panky, Ian."

"No hanky-panky, Kaitlin," he confirmed with a smile on his face.

"I'll be ready when you get here. Goodnight."

"Goodnight, Honey." He could hear her laugh as he hung up the telephone.

It was 8 a.m. when Ian entered the Lawrences' driveway, and Kaitlin was walking out the door. He got out of the car and helped her with her bag of clothes and other things, then asked. "Have you had breakfast yet?"

"Yes. Let's be on the way."

Drenn drove through Charlotte using the expressway and made good time to where he turned off to Cherokee. He checked into the motel at 2 p.m. and declared to himself that he had made good time.

After check-in, they went to eat. They were both starving by that time, so they headed out to the town. They stopped where you could pan for gemstones, and he showed her the difference between a sapphire and a ruby.

Kaitlin and Ian got wet picking out the gemstones from the clear running water, and he loved it.

Next to them were a man and his son. Ian heard the boy talking to his father.

"Dad, all I've got are big rocks." She proceeded to let them tumble away in the water trough.

Ian picked up the so-called rock and immediately recognized it as a ruby or sapphire. "Excuse me, Sir. This looks like a ruby or sapphire. I don't know which, but if you take it inside the office, they'll tell you."

"We'll do that; thank you," he said, and the two of them were off to the office. The rock turned out to be a twelve hundred-carat sapphire, and the boy returned to Ian and thanked him.

"That was a nice thing to do," Kaitlin said to him. He's thoughtful of others.

"You know, Honey, that little boy will think twice before he throws a rock away again. He may even turn out to be a gemologist someday." He laughed.

"What's the purple stuff?" she asked.

"That's amethyst. The larger and darker the stone, the better. Those small pieces aren't any good."

"And where's the gold?"

"In another bag over there." And he pointed to the area where the bags were stored.

"Let's give it a try, Ian," she suggested, and they moved to the area where the bags with a tiny speck of gold in them were being sold.

"Okay, here's how you do it, Kaitlin. Take a small amount of sand and place it in your pan, then add a little water. Work the pan like this." He demonstrated how to shake the pan. "Because the gold is heavier than the sand, it'll fall to the bottom of the pan. Now you want to get rid of the sand by the action of the water and your shaking of the pan. Okay?"

"Got it, Ian." She watched him pan for gold.

"I'm wet all over, Ian. Next time, we should invest in a couple of water-proof aprons." She tried to wipe the wetness away.

"Don't worry about it. You'll dry off, Honey."

Kaitlin quickly mastered how to pan for gold, and after two pans of sand, she suddenly claimed, "There it is! Ian! I've found gold! Look, there it is!" She was jubilant and pointed to a very small piece of gold.

Ian moved closer to her and said, "Yep, that's it. Here, let's put it into this small glass bottle."

She watched as Ian removed the gold from the pan, placed it into a very small water-filled bottle, and then gave it to her. "By the power of the water trough, I hereby dub you a certified gold miner."

She laughed. "Now, where do we get diamonds?" she asked, looking at him.

"Diamonds? We have to go to a location about a hundred miles south-west of Little Rock, Arkansas."

"You're kidding. Diamonds in the United States?" "There's a state park named the US Crater of Diamonds where, for a couple of dollars, you can dig in a specific area for diamonds in the rough. Matter of fact, they use a tractor with a plow to overturn the bare ground for you. I guarantee you will get dirty and may not find anything but dirt."

"Can we go to the US Crater of Diamonds?"

"Yes." He paused. "Ready to get something to eat?"

She nodded and put the small bottle in her pocket. "I'm wet. Can we go back to the motel first? I need to clean up."

"Me too. I'll follow you."

They ate at a restaurant on the north side of Main Street, and Kaitlin proved she was hungry. They finished the dinner with a piece of apple pie and washed it down with hot tea.

"There's a town about twenty miles from here that has a setup similar to what they have here. They have topaz there, which is something you don't find here. Would you like to go there tomorrow morning?"

"What does that do to our travel schedule?"

"We could spend about two hours in Franklin if we leave here at about 8 a.m. And still arrive back home at the scheduled time."

"Ian, can we come back here someday? I really like this place. It's serene, and there's hardly any wind."

"Yes, of course. I like searching for gemstones and gold, and I think you do too."

"I do. Let's go to Franklin when we have more time and Ian, and let's bring a waterproof apron."

"Sounds good to me. Ready to leave?"

"Yes," and she led the way to the car.

In the car, Ian asked her if she would like to take a walk or just go back to the motel. She decided to walk the short distance to the river, only to discover it wasn't as deep as she believed. They held hands like two teenagers and walked there and back.

At the motel, he asked, "Kaitlin, Honey, how does it feel to have me in your bedroom?"

She laughed. "I'm not a virgin, Ian, but it does seem very strange to have a man in my bedroom."

"Look at it this way. You've seen me in my pajamas and think of this as an approval of my new pajamas," he suggested.

"I can hardly wait to see what you're wearing," she said. "What did you do with the others?"

"I had them cleaned and put away until our wedding night." He smiled.

She laughed.

"Are you going to shower before me, or should I go first?"

"I'll shower first. You can have the cold water."

"Thanks. I appreciate that. Are you sure you don't want me to wash your back?" He joked while turning on the radio and finding some decent music.

"In your dreams, Ian Scott Drenn."

Kaitlin had showered and was doing something to her hair when Ian entered the bathroom. He showered, shaved a little closer than normal, and then dressed in his new pajamas. Opening the door, he presented himself for Kaitlin's inspection.

Kaitlin's red hair hung over one eye, but she smiled at him. "Those are better, Dear."

"Do you like the music, Kaitlin?" He acted like he had someone to dance with and waltzed around the room.

She stood, her hair glistening in the light, as she walked over to him. He placed his arm around her waist and brought her closer, then they began to dance, wearing only their pajamas. They said nothing until he kissed her near the end of the song they had danced to.

"I love you, Kaitlin."

"And I love you, Ian Scott Drenn."

Ian carried the luggage to the checkout counter and gave the clerk the room keys. Surprisingly, one of the clerks asked, "Mr. Drenn, what is your wife's name?"

He looked up and smiled. "Her name is Kaitlin Lawrence, the political cartoonist."

About that time, Kaitlin joined Ian, and she heard one clerk say to another, "I told you so."

The other clerk asked Kaitlin, "Ms. Lawrence, may we have your autograph on this cartoon?" and they presented her with one of the cartoons about Ian. "Is your husband the person in the drawings, Ms. Lawrence?"

"Yep," she answered and signed her name.

The two motel clerks were elated and thanked her.

Just before Kaitlin got into the car, Ian said, "You're famous, Honey."

"Yep, thanks to you."

They ate breakfast at the same restaurant where they had eaten dinner the night before. It was exactly nine a.m. when they departed Cherokee, driving the speed limit. Two hours later, Ian and Kaitlin grabbed a snack at a fast-food joint on the west side of Gastonia. That's when the rain started, and Ian slowed down.

Kaitlin had been quiet most of the way, listening to music and writing in her little red notebook. They actually made good time, and Ian pulled into the Lawrences' driveway after five hours and fifteen minutes on a busy road.

She turned to Ian. "How do I tell my mother you and I danced in our pajamas, Ian?"

Ian was getting her suitcase out of the car when he laughed. "Do you tell your mother everything?" They kissed, and Kaitlin opened the door of her house and was met by her mother.

Ian waved and got back into the car. A few minutes later, the car received a twelve-dollar wash job at a place south of Laurinburg.

"Mom, you wouldn't believe it. We danced wearing only our pajamas." Kaitlin was telling her mother while sitting at the kitchen table.

Her mother laughed. "Kaitlin, what am I going to do with you? Wait till I tell your father."

"Mom, we spent one day together, and I learned more about him than I had in the last six months." She sipped tea from her cup. "He's kind, caring, and considerate of other people. He's easy-going, soft-spoken, and has a great sense of humor."

"Does he have a bad side to him? I ask that because you have just described the perfect man, and I know they don't exist, Dear."

"I know that he was a police officer, and I don't think I would want to get on the bad side of him. I remember him telling me once he had to shoot a man to stay alive but couldn't shoot a twelve-year-old boy that shot him."

"Self-discipline is a virtue, Kaitlin. What else happened?"

"When we went to check out, one of the clerks recognized me and asked for my autograph, Mom. My cartoons about Ian and me went statewide. It was funny."

"Don't let that fifteen minutes of fame go to your head, Dear."

"It won't, Mom, but it was strange to have someone ask for my autograph."

"Have you set the date yet?" Her mother was making herself another cup of hot tea.

"We're planning for October 8, but it may be earlier, Mom." She sipped from her teacup.

"Then it's still TBA?"

Kaitlin laughed. "You know, Mom, that's one of the things I like about him. He can produce all kinds of stuff."

"Like a political cartoonist, Dear?"

"I never thought of it that way, but yes."

After five hours on the road and a car clean-up, Ian was ready for a good night's sleep. He thought about dancing with Kaitlin dressed only in her pajamas and what his dance instructor would say, then the sandman visited him.

Chapter Thirteen

riday morning came all too soon. Ian was still in bed when he telephoned Kaitlin. "Good morning. How are you?"

"I'm sitting in the kitchen with my mother."

"Did you tell her about dancing in your pajamas?"

"Yes. She laughed," Kaitlin told him. "What are you doing?"

"I was considering trading the pickup truck this afternoon for something else. Would you like to go shopping?"

"Yes. Are you going to trade the old pickup truck, or are you just going shopping?"

"Just shopping. Why?" He put both feet on the floor.

"Can I drive the T-Bird?"

He laughed. "Sure. Pick you up in an hour?"

"I'll be ready. Bye-bye." She turned to her mother. "We're going shopping for a new pickup truck. I wonder what he's planning?"

"All you have to do is ask him, Dear," her mother suggested as she cleared the kitchen table.

"I've got to get ready," she said as she headed for the bathroom. When she got upstairs, she telephoned Ian. "Ian, can we bring my mother along with us? She needs to get out of the house."

"Sure, but we'll take the Cadillac."

"Okay. Bye-bye."

"See you soon." Drenn hung up the house phone and walked into the bathroom.

Kaitlin returned to the kitchen to find her mother turning on the dishwasher. "Mom, how about coming with Ian and me to shop for a new truck? You need to get out of the house too."

"Are you sure you two don't want to be alone?" She felt the walls were closing in on her and would be happy to go with them.

"No. Ian's okay with it. He says you make tasty tea."

"Tasty tea?" Her mother questioned.

"Yep, that's what he called it."

Mrs. Lawrence laughed. "Okay. I'll go, but I don't know much about shopping for trucks."

"Mom, all you have to know is what color you like and come as you are."

A few minutes later, Ian pulled the Cadillac into the Lawrence driveway and held the doors open for Kaitlin and his future mother-in-law. "Everybody ready? I thought we would hit US 74 and head west."

"Why not north? Fayetteville has many car dealerships," Kaitlin suggested.

"North to Alaska it is." He joked.

"Ian, why are you buying a new pickup truck? Are you planning a trip to Alaska?" Kaitlin asked as they drove north on US 401.

"You like panning for gold, don't you? Well, that's where the gold is."

"You're kidding? When?"

"I don't know, but before, gasoline-operated cars were turned into chicken coops."

"The subject was Alaska, Ian."

"Ah yes, Alaska. I read a book once about a dog named Buck and a gold miner in the Yukon, and it has inspired me to think about searching for gold. I guess that's why I'm shopping for a pickup truck, and there's plenty of gasoline in Canada."

"So why buy it now?"

"I want to ensure it carries only what is needed and there's a specific place for it. The heavier, the more fuel that is used. The lighter, the better."

"That makes sense. Now what color?"

"Color? The one with the best performance and is reliable. We can always paint it later."

"Even pink or purple?" she joked.

"I've got to draw the line on pink. No man would be caught dead in a pink pickup truck." He smiled.

"And what if you never get to go to Alaska?"

"Then we'll paint it pink, and you can drive it!" They laughed.

All afternoon, they went from one dealership to another, and they finally settled on a Ford, Chevrolet, or GMC. With those models in mind, Ian drove south around Raeford and then Laurinburg.

Mrs. Lawrence hadn't said much after a lunch of Bar-B-Q from a place near the fire station on Fort Bragg Road.

"Are you alright, Mom?" Kaitlin asked.

"Yes, but I wonder what your father is going to say when dinner isn't ready."

"I've got a solution, Mom. Don't worry about it." She then turned to Ian. "Ian, would you stop at that Chinese restaurant on South Main Street? They have a delicious rice and chicken plate."

"I know the place. Need any money?"

"No. I've got it." Kaitlin turned back to her mother. "Mom, just tell Dad this is Chinese night."

"That may work, Dear. We'll try it." She smiled at Kaitlin, believing she had solved the problem of dinner.

Ian couldn't find a place to park, so he let Kaitlin out in front of the restaurant while he drove around the block. On his third trip, Kaitlin walked out of the business and was waiting for him at the curb.

Fifteen minutes later, he drove into the Lawrences' driveway and turned off the motor. Mrs. Lawrence was headed for her house before he could open the door for her, and Kaitlin told Ian one of the dinners was for him. He declined dinner with them and drove home after he gave Kaitlin a goodbye kiss.

It had been a long day, and he was tired. He turned on the television and then went to the bathroom, where he washed before eating. The news did nothing to entice him to surf the channels, looking for something better, so he turned the television off.

Thumbing through the mail, he found one bill for heating fuel. Obtaining his checkbook, he wrote out a check and placed it in a return envelope. He will mail it tomorrow. He fell asleep sitting on the sofa that needed to be replaced.

The next morning, he met Kaitlin at the mailbox, and they greeted each other. "Hi, Kaitlin. Did you sleep well?"

"I don't know about you, but I slept like a baby, Ian. All of that shopping got to me, and I know Mom went to bed early last night."

"I slept on the sofa. Someday, I've got to replace that thing," he told her.

"Ian, instead of shopping for a new truck, you should consider buying a new sofa. I sat on it and felt uncomfortable."

"I know. Ready to walk?" He turned north on Purcell Road.

"Let's go, but haven't you forgotten something?" She smiled.

He turned back to her and put one hand around her waist, drawing her closer to him.

Then she said, "You've forgotten to close the door to your house," then laughed and started walking.

He walked over to the side door, closed it, and turned to see Kaitlin walking away from him. "Hey, wait for me!" he yelled. He ran to catch up with her, only to have her start jogging at a slow pace. They jogged to where Purcell Road meets Blue Farms Road, then turned back.

"I received an assignment alert, Ian. That means I will be getting an assignment somewhere soon. What are you going to do?" They continued to walk.

"I'm going to miss you, but there's a friend I attended Richmond Tech with. He is returning from overseas, so I may visit while you're working." They walked on a little further, then he asked, "Do you need anything?"

"No. I'm prepared for just such an assignment."

"Are you prepared for an emergency?"

"Like what?"

"War with China. A flat tire. Being hungry or car trouble," he answered.

"Well, I don't think China will attack until I return. I have a spare tire and a jack and have changed a flat tire before. As for being hungry, you can buy me lunch this afternoon. Anything else, Ian dear."

"What time should I pick you up?" They were at Ian's mailbox. He wrapped his arm around her waist.

"Hmmm, at high noon. I'm hungry." They kissed.

"I'll drive the T-Bird, Honey." They parted, and she started walking toward her home on Purcell Road.

At the Lawrence residence, Mrs. Lawrence was waiting for Kaitlin to finish her walk with Ian. "Kaitlin, your boss has an assignment for you. He gave me this number for you to call." She handed her daughter a slip of notebook paper.

"Thanks, Mom," she said while accepting the slip of paper. A few minutes later, she tells her mother. "Mom, I'm going to Iowa to cover President T's rally! Then they'll have another assignment for me from there."

"Anything I can do to help you?"

"All I have to do is pack this stuff in the car, Mom. Oh, yes. I've got to call Ian." She picked up the house telephone.

"Drenn residence," Ian answered.

"Ian, I've got an assignment, and I must leave now."

"Honey, do your best. Understand?"

"I will. I love you."

"I love you too. Be careful out there."

"I will. Bye-bye." She was walking out the door.

"Bye, Honey." She never heard him.

During the next week, Ian Scott Drenn had the oil changed in his car, made arrangements to purchase a spare tire since new Cadillacs were sold without them, and paid a trip to the police pistol firearms range to practice with his newly purchased Beretta. That took four days, and after that, he was alone.

Chapter Fourteen

At the start of the second week, he got a haircut at Clark's Barber Shop and filled the car with regular gasoline. On Wednesday afternoon, he did another map reconnaissance using a three-year-old Atlas and laid out the dark blue trousers and a light blue striped shirt that he would wear tomorrow. A warm shower and a close shave after eating supper led to a restless night's sleep.

Just before dawn on Thursday morning, Drenn drank a small glass of cold orange juice and ate a slice of toast with cream cheese generously spread on it.

Drenn took the southern route to Florence, South Carolina, where he got onto Interstate Twenty, and on to Atlanta, where he made a short side trip to Georgia's Stone Mountain State Park.

He stopped for the night, west of Birmingham, after refueling and getting something to eat. The traffic was heavy, and he was tired. Sleep came easy.

Friday morning, he had a good breakfast of hotcakes and sausage, topped off with a small glass of cold orange juice. He left Meridian, Mississippi, in good spirits and put his foot extra hard on the gas pedal, only to stop in Vicksburg to visit the National Military Park.

After nine hours of driving, he had to get some rest. He spent Friday night in a motel east of Dallas, and his thoughts turned to Kaitlin and whether he should telephone her or not. He decided not to.

Saturday morning, he calmly drove through heavy Dallas traffic at a moderate speed, keeping up with traffic. His stomach told him it was time for breakfast, so he stopped at a restaurant near Cisco, Texas. He noticed a lot of people were just wandering around doing nothing. A waitress explained to him they were illegal aliens and homeless but didn't speak Spanish, and that alarmed him.

By noon, he was in Odessa and noticed the driver of a dirty white van driving recklessly, weaving back and forth through light traffic. "*What the heck is wrong with that driver?*" he asked himself and turned on his car-mounted cameras. The van struck the sides of three cars, knocking them off the road before it passed him and collided with a car two vehicles ahead of him.

He checked the traffic behind him and saw nothing, then he slammed on his brakes. The cars in front of him bypassed the wreck and kept going.

With his Cadillac in park, he hurried to the car's trunk and retrieved his own emergency kit, then ran to the smashed vehicle.

Ian saw the destroyed blue sedan, with the left door smashed in and broken window glass everywhere. He cleared the left door window of broken glass, only to find Kaitlin with blood on the left side of her head and left arm. He jerked on the crushed door, trying to open it, but the reaction was useless. "Oh, God no!"

He yelled and climbed on top of the wrecked car to reach the sunroof. With a hammer-like tool, he smashed in the glass top and squeezed inside Kaitlin's destroyed car. He cut her seatbelt and tried to move her left leg, but it was nearly impossible, having been caught between the smashed door and the brake pedal.

The smell of gasoline was overpowering, but he worked on freeing her foot until he was forced to cut through the brake pedal with a battery-powered saw he obtained from his emergency kit.

"*She's free!*" he said to himself and tried to push her up through the opening in the sunroof. The fire was spreading fast, and it reached his back. Still, he worked to free her from death.

He saw the blue and white wallet Kaitlin always carried wherever she went burning on the floor of the car, and he grabbed it, burning his right hand in the process. He was successful and placed it inside his heated shirt, then, with all his might, lifted Kaitlin through the sunroof.

Two vehicles from the Texas Department of Public Safety arrived in time to see Ian lay Kaitlin on the ground. One Texas law enforcement officer had radioed for an ambulance and fire truck while Ian rolled onto his back to subdue the heat burning his shirt.

Ian looked back at Kaitlin's burning car, then back at an unconscious Kaitlin. "God help her," he said aloud.

One of the Texas officers approached Ian and Ian asked if he had any oxygen so he could administer it to Kaitlin.

"Are you alright?" The officer asked Ian.

"I'm a little burned on one side, but I'll be okay. It's her I'm worried about. Where will they take her?"

"Odessa Second Avenue Hospital. Here they are now. Don't you want to go with them?" The officer looked at Ian's back.

"No. I'll follow them in my car," Ian said while wrapping a handkerchief around his right hand.

"You know her?"

"Yes. Her name is Kaitlin Lawrence. She's a political cartoonist." The officer was writing all that Ian told him in a report book. "I've got a dash camera in my car. If you want, I can give you a copy of what my camera captured. That may help you."

"Are you in law enforcement?" he asked.

"Medically retired at twenty-four years old," Ian told him. "My name is Ian Scott Drenn." The ambulance had arrived and was taking Kaitlin away. "Got to go. See you at the hospital."

In the ambulance, before arriving at the hospital, Kaitlin awoke. "My leg hurts, my head hurts, my arms hurt. Am I okay?"

One of the Emergency Medical Technicians answered her. "What's your name?"

"My name is Kaitlin Lawrence. Where are we?" She started to feel the left side of her head but was stopped.

"You are in an ambulance, and we're taking you to a hospital. You're going to be alright."

At the Second Avenue Hospital, Ian pulled into the emergency room entrance and met the Texas law officer. "Have you got a phone I can download this information on?" Ian asked.

"Let me see it first, then, if applicable, you can download a copy for me." "That's reasonable. Playing," and Ian turned on the camera screen for the officer to watch. A minute later, the officer confirmed that he would like to have a copy.

Ian made him a copy of the situation that hurt many lives and depicted his own part in it.

"Mister Drenn, I wish we had more travelers such as yourself. It would make my job a whole lot easier. Here's my calling card. You need me. Call me."

"Thanks, Officer," Ian looked at the card. "Officer Gomez," he said, turning away and opening the trunk of his car. There he obtained a clean t-shirt and dress shirt, then walked into the Emergency Room reception area. His shirt was nearly burned to rags, and his right hand had second-degree burns, but he held back the pain.

Their Emergency Room was extremely busy, but he found the room where Kaitlin was being treated and stood by the door.

When Kaitlin was removed from the operating room, Ian asked the person he believed was the doctor, "How is she, Doctor?"

"Who?" he asked. "I don't know her name."

"Her name is Kaitlin Lawrence. She's a political cartoonist. Her father's an orthopedic surgeon."

"How do you know this?"

"I live just down the block from her. My name is Ian Drenn."

"Are you family?"

"No, but I can telephone her parents. The first question they will want to know is your name or a point of contact, sir."

"She's going to be alright. There was no concussion. Broken left ankle. Cuts on her left arm and the left side of her head. You notify the parents because I'm up to my ears in patients tonight."

"Thanks, Doctor." Ian backed away from him and sought a quiet place to call Kaitlin's mother and father.

"Mrs. Lawrence, this is Ian Scott Drenn. I'm in Odessa, Texas. Kaitlin was involved in a car accident and is in the hospital. She has a broken left ankle and cuts on her left arm and the left side of her head. There was no concussion. The doctor said she will recover, and then I can see her." He could hear Mrs. Lawrence crying, and when Mister Lawrence came on the telephone, Ian repeated all that he had told Mrs. Lawrence and gave him a point of contact.

"I'll be here, Mister Lawrence. I was on my way to Peoria, Arizona. I had no idea where Kaitlin was. All I knew was that she was on assignment, Sir." Ian received instructions on what to do, and he agreed to them. "Good night, Sir."

Ian was finally attended to and treated for his burns, and he was discharged shortly after. He stayed in the waiting area for Kaitlin, with others doing the same thing.

The following morning, one of the nurses informed him he could see her. He walked into her room and saw her smile. It wasn't a big smile, and the first thing she wanted to know was where he came from.

"I was two cars behind you and saw the van driving you off the road. Got everything on my car cameras. Followed the ambulance here. Oh, one thing else. I telephoned your parents, and they asked me to let them know when I got to see you. So would you like to call them or should I?"

"I'll call them," he said as he handed her his phone. "You want some privacy?"

"No. Stay." She punched in her telephone number, and her mother answered.

Ian could hear only one side of the conversation but imagined what her mother was saying.

"I'm okay, Mom. Ian is here, and he'll take good care of me." She listened. "I don't know when I'll leave here, but I'll know something after the doctor's visit." She listened. "I'll let you and Dad know what happens, Mom." She listened. "Okay, Mom. Bye-bye." Kaitlin handed the telephone back to Ian.

Ian attempted to take it with his right hand, then remembered the bandage and took it with his left hand.

"Why the bandage, Ian? What happened?"

"I burned my hand, but it's a minor injury, Honey." Then he remembered. "I saved this from the car." He handed her the partially burned blue and white wallet after removing it from his shirt pocket.

She took the wallet and then smelled it. "It's burnt. Did my car burn?"

"It's a cinder block, Kaitlin. Nothing survived, Honey."

"Nothing?" She looked at her wallet.

"Nothing," he repeated. "Accept your wallet, and it's just a little singed on one side. If you want, I can show you pictures."

"My clothes, my artwork, my purse?"

"Nothing. It's a piece of molded steel and plastic, Kaitlin."

"If it's that bad, how did you save my wallet?"

"I grabbed it while it was burning because I believed you would need it," he told her.

About that time, a nurse entered the hospital room. "The doctor will be here soon. Do you have someone to care for you?" she asked.

"Yes," Kaitlin answered. "He's right here." She looked at Ian, and he confirmed what she had told the nurse.

Five minutes later, the doctor entered the hospital room and stared at Ian. "Drenn?"

"Yes, Sir."

"How's the back?"

"Doing good, Sir."

"You know this young lady?"

"Yes, Sir. Hope to marry her one of these days, Sir."

He laughed and looked at Kaitlin. "How's the ankle?"

"There's no feeling, Doctor." He examined her head and arm. "Are you getting any headaches or numbness?"

"No, Sir. Just a little hungry."

"Well, we serve good food here, but I think you can go home." He turned to Ian. "Drenn, can you take care of her?"

"Yes, Sir."

"Nurse, let's discharge her this afternoon after she eats." He smiled at the nurse.

"Yes, Sir," and she wrote something on her clipboard, then exited the room.

"Drenn, Gomez said you were a former law enforcement officer and saved this young lady's life. I understand he's recommending you for a commendation. I'm proud to add my name to the recommendation."

Ian Scott Drenn was surprised, and all he could say was, "Thank you, Sir." He watched the doctor leave Kaitlin's room and waited for her to say something.

"Ian Scott Drenn. Explain, please." Kaitlin said in a forceful-sounding plea.

"Gomez was the Texas Department of Public Safety officer on the scene. He's the one who radioed for an ambulance and fire truck," he explained.

"I wasn't talking about Officer Gomez. I was talking about you."

"I didn't know it was you in the car that was broad-sided. I stopped, got you out of the car and the ambulance brought you here."

"You forgot the part where the car was on fire and your back and hand were burned," she added.

"I completely forgot that your foot was held in place by the brake pedal and the crushed door. I cut the brake pedal away but had to break your ankle to release it from the crushed side of the door."

"You broke my ankle!" She couldn't believe it.

"Yes. Shoot me if you want to!"

She laughed. "Why?"

"It was either that or let you burn to death, and I wasn't going to let that happen."

"What am I going to do with you?"

"The question is this. Why do you smell like burnt gasoline, and where am I going to get you some new clothes?" He smiled.

"I thought that smell was coming from you and didn't want to say anything about it."

"I suggest we go to the neighborhood medical supply store and get you a wheelchair. Then to a department store for something to wear. I have a feeling you want to continue your assignment, and a broken ankle isn't going to stop you."

"I was thinking about it," she willingly confessed.

"All you need is reliable transportation, which I have. Clothes, which I can purchase. Money to survive on, which I have. Art supplies, which you will have to pick out. And what else?"

"And you to love me," she said.

"Honey, you don't have to worry about that because I love you and your broken ankle." He saw tears welling up in her eyes. "Hey," he said, moving closer to her, "no tears, Honey. You'll get the pillow wet." He tried to be funny.

She put her arms around him. "I love you, Ian Scott Drenn."

"And you know I love you, and guess what?"

"What?" she whispered.

"Your lunch is here," he announced.

She laughed.

Chapter Fifteen

Two long hours after Kaitlin ate lunch, she was granted permission to leave the hospital. Ian paid the bill, and Kaitlin was put in a wheelchair and then pushed to Ian's nearby Cadillac.

Their first stop took them to Bill's Bicycle Shop, where Ian purchased a bicycle rack and attached it to the car trunk. Now, he had a place to put the collapsible wheelchair.

They just made it in time to the medical appliance shop, where Ian purchased a used wheelchair. Kaitlin was now highly mobile and could store the crutch.

An open sporting goods store provided clothing for Kaitlin, but the left leg had to be slightly modified with a pair of sharp scissors.

Dillion's Department Store furnished the clothing, underwear, cosmetics, luggage, and everything else Kaitlin needed.

By the time they located an art supply store, it was closed. "How about something to eat, Kaitlin?"

"Let's get some fast food and take it back to the motel. I'm hungry and tired and need to rest."

At the Super 12 Motel, Ian parked the Cadillac near Room 7. Then he got out of the car, opened the door, and then returned for Kaitlin. He gently picked her up and carefully carried her inside, putting her on a soft bed. Next, he retrieved the wheelchair and placed the fast food on it. Kaitlin was waiting for him to help her sit in the wheelchair.

"Honey, do you want to sleep, or should I wash you?"

"You shower while I rest, then I'll wash. I want to get rid of this smell."

"Same here." When Ian finished eating, he showered and shaved, then changed into his multi-colored pajamas, which had kangaroos and koalas on them. When Kaitlin saw them, all she could do was laugh.

"I might have known you would wear something like that!" Kaitlin was feeling better.

"I bought these at Ward's, and yes, they were on sale. I thank you." Ian smiled and was elated to see Kaitlin happy. "Are you ready for a wash-down?"

"I can't get this cast wet for the next few days, Ian. So please be careful."

"Would you mind if I put your cast into a clean new trash bag? That way, no water will get on it." He held up a plastic trash bag for her to see.

"That's pragmatic, Ian. Go ahead." She watched Ian place the bag around her cast, then said, "I'll take it from here. If I need you, I'll call."

"Okay. I'm here for you."

Ian turned on the television, then stretched out on the bed, waiting for Kaitlin to call him. His eyes were almost closed when Kaitlin said she needed his help.

"Would you wash my back, please?"

Ian poured a generous amount of liquid soap on her washcloth and washed her back using a circular motion, then rinsed the cloth a couple of times to get the soap out of it. Finally, he finished.

"That's it, Kaitlin. Want me to dry it?"

"Yes, thank you." She smiled at the gentleness she felt in his hands and gave him the towel. "Okay. Now the left leg, please. My leg is difficult to lift from the sitting position," she explained. "But don't go too high up the leg, Ian."

He started washing the left leg with the same speed and pressure he had applied to her back, maybe a little higher, but the job was done, and Kaitlin liked it.

She easily slipped into a pink nylon gown that Ian said he liked, and then he wheeled her out to her bed.

"They have a microwave oven here. How about a bag of popcorn to munch on?"

"And where are you going to get popcorn?" she asked.

"From Ian Scott Drenn's Magic Survival Kit. That's where…" He held up two small bags of microwavable popcorn removed from his green overnight bag.

She laughed and nodded her head, approving the popcorn.

They spent the rest of the evening sitting close to each other, munching on popcorn, sipping cold Coke, and watching television. Just before they settled in for the night, Kaitlin turned to him and said, "Ian, you've been very considerate of me and my work. I want this assignment to be my last, and I don't think we should wait any longer to be married."

"Are you sure this is what you want? If it is, give it all you've got and be proud of your work, Honey."

"I'm sure."

"Where do you want to be married?"

"Don't laugh. At the Republican Party's meeting house on June 17, we'll invite all Republicans." He kissed her.

"And we can have the reception there?"

"Yep. Keep it simple." She kissed him.

"And the honeymoon in Hawaii?"

"Yep. I've always wanted to go to Hawaii." He kissed her, and she returned the kiss.

"And when we return, maybe we can help each other with something I've been working on. You see, I've been writing these open letters to the public expressing the actions of an anti-American Socialist-Democrat tiger that roams the areas around Laurinburg and Rockingham. He meets the local citizens who don't want to give up their firearms. My question is. Can you draw a tiger?"

"Let me read one of your open letters so I can get the feel of what I'm drawing. Then I can give you a better answer." She was very much interested in his project.

Ian readily handed her two sheets of college-ruled, loose-leaf notebook paper. She read.

Open Letter #3

Dear Sons and Daughters,

Once upon a time, an arrogant Socialist-Democrat tiger prowled Highway US 74 leading to the town of Rockingham. Along the way, he would growl at people passing by, and they would cringe at the very sound and smell of him.

He came to a nationwide chain store. "I've come for your guns and ammunition," he told the store manager.

"Yes. Please come in. Take all you want."

The tiger smiled. "This will make you safe," the tiger gladly offered. "The government will keep you well protected."

Outside the store, the tiger observed a disabled man wearing one tan desert boot slowly making his way across a cemetery. "Do you have a gun?" the tiger asked.

"No," said the man with one tan desert boot. "You should see McQueen. He lives just north of here. In Ellerbe." He pointed north.

Finally, the tiger came to a mailbox with McQueen's name on it. Behind the house was a pond. The tiger decided to get some fish to eat. Just as the tiger dipped his paw into the pond, he heard a door open and turned to see McQueen. He gasped. McQueen was dressed in his best bib overalls and wore a clean white shirt, Mrs. McQueen had washed and ironed on Saturday morning. In his hands was the biggest twelve-gauge double-barreled shotgun he had ever seen.

"I've come to take your guns," the tiger bravely told him.

"Is your hospital insurance paid up?" McQueen grumbled.

"Why?" asked the now-cautious tiger.

"Because I'm going to fill your backside with buckshot unless you get away from my fishpond."

"The government will keep you safe," the tiger moaned.

"Listen, Tiger. The founders of this great nation were well-read historians. They knew the surest and quickest way to conquer a people was to disarm them. Socialism has never brought prosperity! Socialism is a problem, not a solution! Socialism/Marxism/Communism is not a step forward! It is twenty steps backward!"

The tiger was getting worried now and turned to run.

McQueen was a man of few words. He fired from the hip. You could see the fur fly as the tiger ran for cover.

The moral of this story is:

If you want McQueen's shotgun, you should never try to steal his fish.

Love,

Dad

Kaitlin had a smirk on her face when she handed the papers back to Ian. "I think I can produce something. But you will have to continue the storyline."

"I can do that. At least until the election is over," he admitted. "Ready for me to turn the television off?"

"Yep. I'm tired, but you could rub my back. Just a little?"

"Turn over." Kaitlin laid her head on the soft, white pillow and pulled the cover up to her waist.

Ian used his right hand and tenderly massaged her back, following the muscle outline. Gently moving up and down her back, his rubbing turned into a caress, and Kaitlin liked it. It didn't take long for her to fall asleep, and Ian moved back to his bed.

Ian remembered where the art supply store was and found a nearby place to eat a late breakfast. Since he was parked on the same block, he merely pushed her to where she could do some shopping.

Once she introduced herself, the sales representative realized she was a professional artist and understood what Kaitlin wanted. They were out of the place in thirty minutes and on the way to a late lunch in eastern El Paso.

Ian and Kaitlin spent the night in Tucson's Motel 12. After they ate a light dinner and Kaitlin got a back rub, they got a good night's rest.

The following morning, Ian had the Cadillac thoroughly cleaned and refueled. While Kaitlin patiently waited, she read the local newspaper and talked about Ian's other written open letters to the public.

Entering Phoenix on Interstate 10, Ian obtained a motel room, and Kaitlin directed him to turn north on Sixty-Seventh Street, then right on Cactus Avenue. It's the third house on the right. He was in Peoria, and he knew it because the individual he was going to visit resided in the same area. If, in fact, it was the same house.

Kaitlin used Ian's telephone to call her friend Jodi, and she was at the door waiting for the evergreen Cadillac to show up.

Jodi instantly came to the car door, and Kaitlin opened it while Ian was getting the wheelchair from the bicycle rack. They hugged each other and were talking when Ian picked her up and put her in the wheelchair.

Kaitlin started to introduce Ian to her when she quickly went to him, and they hugged. "Do you know Ian?" Kaitlin asked.

Jodi turned back to Kaitlin. "He was Tom's best man at our wedding right out of Richmond Tech, Kaitlin. I thought you knew."

"Where's Tom?" he asked Jodi.

"He's getting the car refueled and should be back in a moment, Ian. Let's go inside."

Ian cautiously pushed Kaitlin's wheelchair into the house, and Kaitlin said she could take over from there. Ian told her he would be on the front porch, and if she needed him, all she had to do was call. He smiled at Jodi and closed the door behind him.

He could hear the two of them laughing and talking. Tom returned home and saw Ian sitting on the front porch. They shook hands and talked about Hawaii, their jobs, and the accident until Kaitlin and Jody came out of the house. Jodi introduced her to her husband, and Kaitlin told him about how she came to be in a wheelchair.

"We must be leaving, Tom," Ian said. "Kaitlin decided to work tomorrow, and she must get ready." He then turned to Jodi and said, "It was nice seeing you again, Jodi."

She hugged him and said, "Come back soon, Ian. You and Kaitlin make a good pair."

"Thanks. See you later."

"Take good care of her."

"I'll try, but she's a handful," he joked.

On the way back to the motel, Kaitlin suggested they get something to eat, and Ian stopped at the first place Kaitlin said was acceptable.

Back at the motel, Kaitlin told Ian she wanted to wear her white blouse with a blue trim and blue pants tomorrow. He hung them up in the small, open closet to get the wrinkles out of it. He did the same for his own clothing and attempted to match it with the same colors.

"The rally starts at 1 p.m., Ian. How far are we from Great Canyon University?"

"About a half hour's drive. Depending on traffic," he answered while sitting on his bed, looking at a map of Phoenix.

"I need to talk to John Dickerson there. He's one of President T's assistants for events like this. He'll tell me where to be during the rally," she explained. "So, we should leave here by 11 a.m."

"Do you want to have breakfast before going?" He waited for her to say something. "I asked that because I spotted a fast-food joint where we could eat near here."

"Okay." She thought for a second. "You know, Jodi asked me why we're not having sex, and all I could do was laugh." Kaitlin seemed to be considering something else to say but didn't.

"Kaitlin," he gently took her hands into his and said, "When we have sex, it's going to mean something special. It's just not going to be something to do. Right?"

"Right. Something we can build on in the future, Ian. But then again." Ian's ears perked up, and she teasingly laughed. "Time for a bath, Ian."

"I can tie the trash bag around your cast if you want to try and shower, Honey."

"I'll need help getting into and out of the tub," she told him. "I'll wear my robe in, and once in, I'll hand it to you. Got it?"

"I understand. May I take pictures?" He laughed.

"No! But then again," she playfully teased.

Ian could hear her cheerfully singing in the shower, indicating she was in good spirits, and he liked that. Then she turned off the shower water and called for him. "Robe, please."

Ian attentively handed her the white chenille robe and then carefully helped her out of the shower to take her place in the wheelchair. She noted Ian had placed a red velvet cushion on the seat, making it a little more comfortable for her. She smiled, thinking he was extremely thoughtful about her situation. She felt his hands remove the trash bag from around her cast. "Thank you, Dear," she said and proceeded to thoroughly dry herself after Ian left the bathroom. Afterward, she put on a light blue gown with white trim.

"You look great," Ian complimented her. "Rub down?"

"Yes, I like your hands on my back."

The next morning, Ian woke up early and shaved, showered, and dressed for all but his shirt. He knelt down close to Kaitlin's head and placed his cheek next to hers.

"You know how to awaken a girl, Ian." She smiled and snuggled close to him.

"Time to get up, Honey." He softly whispered in her ear.

"Just a few more minutes, Dear," she answered, cuddling closer to him.

It was almost 10 a.m., and Kaitlin was hungry before they arrived at a nearby restaurant.

At the Great Canyon University, Ian found a place to park near the entrance to the auditorium. He pushed Kaitlin's wheelchair inside, only to be met by a Security Officer. After Kaitlin produced her identification and the Security Officer found her name on the Media List, they were allowed to enter. Ian received a guest visitor identification badge from the Security Officer.

Kaitlin met with John Dickerson, and he guided them to an area reserved for the media. Out of the blue, Kaitlin turned to Ian and said she didn't want to go to Hawaii for a honeymoon.

"Is it that you don't want to go to Hawaii, or you don't want a honeymoon?" Ian asked and eagerly waited for an answer.

"I don't want to wait to go to Hawaii. Let's get out of here. I want a life with you."

Ian smiled and handed his identification badge back to the puzzled Security Officer on their way out. "*Love never dies,*" Ian thought to himself. They helped Tom and Jodi Spevere celebrate their third anniversary before leaving Peoria, resulting in photographs being taken, handshakes, and hugs. Ian turned the evergreen-colored Cadillac east after Kaitlin kissed him on the cheek.

"You know what, Kaitlin? We should replace that old sofa."

She laughed and laughed and laughed some more. "*They would have a good life together,*" she thought. "I love you, Ian Scott Drenn."

The End

About the Author

George E. Boyer came to North Carolina via the US Army Special Forces from Terre Haute, Indiana, in 1955.

He graduated from Monterey Peninsula College, California, and attended Campbell College, North Carolina, plus a course in spoken Russian.

After retirement from the Army, he worked in Maxton as a Job Counselor and as a Correctional Officer in Wagram. Then in the Middle East, as an Intelligence Officer in the Multinational Force & Observers.

In 1965, he married Geneva Priest Henderson, and they raised three daughters. Debbie and Marie died of cancer, while Cindy lives nearby and is of immense value. Marie and Cindy are published authors in their own right. Geneva was an insurance representative in Fayetteville, then worked at Bill's Cleaners before retiring.

He has also authored *Emmett's Militia*, *Bronski's Storm*, and *The Chalk Maker Cometh*.

Editor's Review

"This is a captivating romantic story mixed with a bit of politics. The language is simple to grasp, and the plot is engaging."

Jessie Raymond (UK)

Made in the USA
Middletown, DE
26 September 2023

39431471R00070